ANGELA J. FORD

BETRAYED BRIDES

# MAGE
# BRIDE

*For romantasy readers. This one is for you. Enjoy this mash-up that's part fantasy, part romance and part mystery.*

# The Disappearance

The warmth of the fire lured her closer, hands outstretched, stocking feet up on tiptoes to ensure not a sound was made. The babe had fought his exhaustion with every breath in his body, his cries sounding like yells, tiny fists pumping the air until, at last, he gave up. She was relieved to lay him down, head throbbing with the beginnings of a headache, arms sore from bouncing him.

She loved the comforting scent of him, the downy fluffy hair on his head, the softness of his chubby cheeks, the way those dark eyes grinned at her. But he took up so much of her time, she just needed a few moments to turn her attention elsewhere.

The kettle on top of the fire boiled, sending a spray of liquid into the fire. It hissed back as though the two were having a spat, kettle versus fire, even though they both needed each other.

A sour smell came, almost rotten and burnt. A sigh left her lips. Was the soup burned again? Her hungry husband would complain, and this time, he'd probably follow through on his threat to bring his mother to the house to cook and clean for them, at least while the baby was young. But she didn't want a mother-in-law underfoot, lording over her. She'd gotten married for independence, to run her own home and start a family of her own. But she wasn't good at either these days.

Wrapping her hands in her skirt, she stepped toward the fire. Light shone on her long, sleek hair, revealing shades of dark red, highlighting the golden-brown hues of her dark skin. She sniffed as she approached the fire, brows knitting together. The rotten scent was stronger and less of a burnt smell, but a sulfuric, gagging odor.

A shadow moved behind her and fear leaped into her throat. Snatching up the ladle, she spun to face the intruder, only to discover herself alone in the two-room hut, the ladle above her head like a weapon, the shadow, her own.

Pressing her hand to her heart, she returned to the fire, shaking her head at her own stupidity. The wind always howled like a murderous beast this time of year, but it was dark and she was not used to being alone. The rough day with the babe and the idea of her mother-in-law moving in rattled her nerves.

Removing the lid from the pot, she stirred the stew, but the aroma of beef chunks and vegetables wasn't enough to dispel the strange scent. *Where was it coming from?*

Suddenly, there was heat on the back of her neck and the heavy musk of an animal filled her nose. The ladle crashed to the floor with a bang, but the baby, heavy in the embrace of sleep, didn't stir. A furry arm came around her waist and snatched her against a hard body. A scream wailed up her throat as she was yanked backward. The air gave a shiver and she vanished.

The fire leaped up, lapping at the contents of the spilled stew, then resettled into an easy rhythm. Golden flames illuminated the empty hut, the sleeping babe, the ladle in front of the fire. . .and something else.

Where the woman once stood were glowing runes, burned into the stone floor.

# Phera

A scream of horror died in my throat as I bolted upright, sending the bed covers tumbling onto the floor. Pressing a hand to my thumping heart, I took deep gulps of thick air to calm myself. Menacing golden eyes flashed in my memory, and I fought to keep the cloying panic down.

It was only a dream. A nightmare. The monster wasn't real.

But it felt real, the type of dream that was so intense, so realistic it lingered, imprinted on one's memory like a bad omen. I almost felt searing heat blooming across my bare shoulders and claws digging into my side hard enough to draw blood. Yet it was only a dream. There was no monster with golden eyes and curled horns meant for impaling, for monsters did not exist in the known lands. I was safe in the Academy of Mages.

Even as the icy grip of the nightmare faded, reality sank in and I lurched out of bed, only to be dragged back by the heavy manacles around one leg. The plain decor of the windowless room left me feeling suffocated, but in reality, it was the runic silver bracelets around my ankles and wrists that made me feel trapped because they suppressed my magic.

I was a prisoner in the Academy of Mages, and today, my fate would be determined.

A tap came at the door and I spun to face it, my fingers going to my black curls. Usually, I preferred my appearance to be impeccable, my honey brown skin glowing with health, my glossy black curls tamed to fall gracefully around my shoulders, and the clothing that draped my willowy frame stylish yet modest. Being a prisoner and worrying myself sick hadn't done me any favors. I felt—and likely looked—much older than my twenty-five years.

The door was an invisible slit in the wall which opened with magic, and only the guards knew the magical words to open the holding cells. Since I was a prisoner waiting for my sentence, the mages imprisoned me in the Academy of Mages instead of deep in the dungeons. Were they coming already? The lack of windows in the room made it difficult to tell time, yet it seemed early for them to come for me. I wasn't ready. Truth be told, I'd never be ready.

The door slid open and a ball of bright colors burst inside, hurling across the room toward me. It took a full moment to ensure my eyes weren't betraying me before surprise propelled me forward.

"Lessie!" I gasped as my best friend embraced me. Tight. "How are you here? You're supposed to be in the floating city, not here."

"I came as soon as I heard," Lessie announced, releasing me only enough to look at my face. "I'm so sorry, Phera. I never imagined they'd detain you like this."

Shame washed over me but I held her gaze, keeping my voice low. "They were right to detain me, Lessie. I broke the law. I knew what I was doing and did it anyway."

"Surely no. Phera! If what you say is true, they'll take your magic. They'll take everything from you."

Letting go of her, I rubbed at my wrists. "All my hopes are pinned on the hearing, that the judges will be sympathetic. I only used dark magic for the greater good."

Lessie's mouth turned down. "I want to hear the entire story in your own words."

"If we have time, I'll tell you, but Lessie, you shouldn't be here. I don't want to get you into trouble because of what I've done."

"Nonsense." Lessie sniffed and hefted a bag onto the bed. "I brought clothes. You can't wear a prisoner's garb to the hearing. They'll judge you right away. A modest dress, nothing too revealing, and your hair neatly done will go a long way. Who is representing you?"

I held her gaze, even though I wanted to look away, to sink into my shame. "No one. I used blood magic, Lessie. There's no defense for it."

Lessie sat down heavily on the bed, as though all the breath had been drained from her body. "It's worse than I thought," she moaned.

"But the academy knows me," I protested, clinging to gossamer threads of hope. "I began my training at eighteen and I studied here for four years. All the mages can vouch for my character. I've only been gone three years. I'm still the same person."

Lessie squeezed my hand, tears shining in her bright brown eyes. "I hope you're right. I hope they see it that way. Using dark magic, blood magic, is unforgivable. Our studies here at the academy taught us about corruption and darkness and sorcery. They won't forgive you outright."

"I've thought of that." I squirmed, taking my hand

out of hers to hug myself. The magical bracelets banged together with a loud clanging sound. I winced. "The most I can hope for is to avoid the dungeons, and the ability to work myself back into their good graces. Remember when we first began our studies? A woman named Chiny worked here. No one paid her much attention, but I discovered that she'd been a mage. Her magical powers were suppressed—I don't know why— but instead of being punished in the dungeons, she served her sentence as a prisoner in the academy, working off her years of service. They gave her a chance. Why not me?"

Lessie leaned back on her elbows, one foot tapping against the stones. Her eyes narrowed as she calculated my options. "True, we don't know what she did to gain such a light sentence. I'm afraid, Phera, terrified for you. If given the opportunity, I'll speak out and vouch for you with everything I have. But answer me this, are you remorseful at all? If you had the chance to go back, would your actions be different?"

I pressed my lips together. It was one question I'd wrestled with on endless nights. I had broken the sacred code that all mages adhered to, but it was out of desperation. My words turned vicious when I spoke. "I stopped a horrible, terrible, dangerous person, and I'd do so again in a moment."

Lessie pressed a hand to her head. "That's what I'm afraid of. Phera, your zeal is admirable, but this time, you went too far. Never let the court know you aren't sorry and don't get that look on your face. They'll lock you in the deepest, darkest dungeon and slay the only person with the magical code to set you free."

I nodded. "I was reckless and got caught. It won't happen again."

Lessie sighed. "I believe you, but will they?"

I already knew the answer to that question. Despite the firmness in my tone when I spoke to Lessie, everything inside of me was silently screaming. In one moment, I'd thrown away my entire life and the idea of never using magic again or of being locked away was overwhelming. I didn't want her to see how frightened I was, so I turned my back to her, throat raw, tears burning the back of my eyes.

Lessie, sensing my needs, stood and opened the bag. "Let's get you ready."

It was one thing to be brave with Lessie, alone in my cell, but quite another to hold my head high in front of the entire assembly. Those gathered included renowned mages from across the known world, instructors from the Academy of Mages, and a few rows of students, pen and paper in hand, ready to "learn" from the proceedings. Head high, I walked past the rows of gossiping mouths to my seat at the front bench. The judge's pulpit was empty, but the governing committee of mages—my judges—took their seats on stage. Some of them had traveled far to be here, hence why I'd been locked up for a few weeks—to give everyone ample time to arrive.

I was grateful to sit down, and even though the guards had separated Lessie and me, just knowing she'd forsaken her post and traveled back to support me gave me strength. But not enough. All the hope and bravery I'd had speaking with her faded under the sharp glares of those assembled. I'd get the maximum sentence, and just the thought of being locked away made a sharp pain climb up my belly. The judgmental whispers and open stares of disbelief made me want to sink into the floor. I couldn't do this.

The gavel banged down on the pulpit and Mage Margot rose to her feet. She was one of the instructors at the academy and had been there for decades. She was a small woman, only five feet tall, with bird-like bones, but her presence commanded attention. Although she was blind, she had a keen sense about her, and now her commanding tone boomed across the auditorium. "All rise for Lord Pieter."

Lord Pieter strode in from the back of the room, walking the length of it, his deep-purple robes billowing out behind him. A thick, black beard and mustache covered most of his expression and bushy eyebrows hid his deep-set eyes. He was known for his firm yet fair judgments, but my heart still faltered when he took his place behind the pulpit and those dark eyes examined me. Regret washed over me. He was one elder I regretted disappointing. When I'd graduated from the academy, he'd shaken my hand and told me I showed great promise.

I'd dashed those dreams to dust. It wasn't any easier with Mage Margot either. Even though she couldn't look me in the eye, I sensed her disapproval from the bench. Pressing my hands together, I kept my back straight and fixed my gaze on a speck of peeling plaster on the wall.

Lord Pieter cleared his throat, causing a reverent silence to hang over the assembly. "Today, we have gathered to pass judgment on the case of Mage Phera and the use of dark magic, which is forbidden to all mages. Such an act is unforgivable and requires the most severe punishment. Let me be clear. What was done was unacceptable and if those of you gathered here should know that any attempt to use dark magic, even though the intention may be for good, shall come under the authority of this court. Yesterday, I was willing to hear witnesses and testimony to this case. However, as of early this morning, everything has changed."

*What had changed?* My mouth went numb, and despite my intention to remain focused and calm, my gaze moved from the peeling plaster to his face. I squeezed my fingers together, trying with all my strength to keep my leg from bouncing up and down with anxiety. It sounded as though he intended to be lenient and hear my side of the story, but now judgment would come fast and heavy. I was to be an example of what happened to mages who stepped out of line.

"Last night, we received an urgent and surprising message from the Ice Lords of the North."

Lord Pieter paused, knowing the impact of his word. A ripple of surprised murmurs burst through the crowd. I frowned, wishing I could turn around to see Lessie's expression. *What did the ice lords have to do with me?*

We knew little about them and their lifestyles. I'd heard the words *savage* and *uncultured* used when speaking of them, but in truth, ice lords kept to themselves, willing to live on the edges of the unknown lands. They refused to trade or permit mages to set foot in their land. In accordance with the peace treaty, the ice lords kept an outpost, used for communication. However, no mage had set foot there in decades.

Diplomacy required that the ice lords remain in the good graces of the governors of Ethunia, the southern lands. After all, they had signed the peace agreement, although it came with strict stipulations that no mage was to enter their lands unless explicitly invited. And that explicit invitation had never come.

In historical studies at the academy, there was debate on why the ice lords kept their land closed to others. There was speculation that, despite signing the treaty, the ice lords lived in direct contradiction of the policies and practices they were supposed to uphold. I was never interested in why, because there were much loftier placements to vie for. Every mage competed for placement in highly desired countries across the known world of Ethunia.

But ice lords? Dread coursed through my veins as Lord Pieter continued to speak and the murmurs of surprise brought on by his announcement died down.

"For the first time in our history, the Ice Lords of the North have requested a mage or two to assist them in a delicate matter concerning life and death. At the Academy of Mages, we aim to uphold law and order and maintain peace across Ethunia. The ice lords have made it known that this is a case which threatens peace and jeopardizes the work we've done throughout the decades. Because they are part of the known lands and have signed the peace treaty, this is a request we cannot deny. Therefore, mages will be appointed to assist them in their time of need."

Lord Pieter paused again, giving time for more argumentative conversation to take place in the assembly. But I wished he'd go on. A buzzing had started in my ears and a terror gripped me. A sneaking suspicion was taking hold, but I wanted him to speak, to clarify what he was asking—or rather, demanding.

"Placement is important here. As mages, your position in this world is critical and the country you serve gives you power far beyond your magic. A placement with the ice lords is not an elevation of a career but a degradation, a punishment."

His eyes locked on mine, and a silent scream began in my mind.

*No.*

*No, no, no, no, no!*

Lord Pieter picked up the gavel. "Mage Phera, please stand."

A wave of faintness came over me, but I managed to stand firm in front of my elders, my instructors, my peers, and mages who were once my friends. This was humiliation at its finest.

"Phera, your title of mage has been stripped and your magic has been suppressed for purposefully indulging in dark magic. Your intent is not pertinent and does not matter. You knew the laws of this land and you willfully ignored them. I hereby sentence you to ten years in the dungeons or ten years serving the ice lords on the edges of the unknown lands. It is your choice."

Ten years. The longevity of the term rang in my mind. My mouth opened, yet no words came out. I swallowed and tried again as the assembly waited, all eyes on me.

"I will serve the ice lords."

# Phera

The guards escorted me out among the uproar of protests, the banging of the gavel, and the chants of the students. I didn't know whether they agreed or disagreed with my sentence, I was just grateful to get out of there. More than anything, I wanted to sink into a hot bath and wash my skin clean from their judging eyes. But it was not to be. The guards escorted me back to the holding cell and left me to pace, back and forth, this time without being chained to the bed—apparently now that I was sentenced to the north, no one had a care. But I had questions—many questions I suspected would remain unanswered.

I waited for details on when I'd be leaving and what I needed to take with me while speculating on Lord Pieter's words. He hadn't said that I'd be free to practice magic while assisting the ice lords, but the fact that they explicitly requested mages indicated they expected magic. My hands went to my wrists and I ran my fingers over the runes on the bracelets.

A tap came at the door and a moment later, it swung open. I faced it, expecting to see one of the mages, but instead, Lessie burst inside again. This time, she shut the door carefully behind her and approached me, a strange expression on her face.

"Lessie, what is it?"

She sat down on the bed and dropped her head into her hands. After a moment of silence, she sat up, facing me. "I spoke with Lord Pieter and Mage Margot. They agreed I can go with you."

My jaw dropped. "Lessie, no. You can't throw your life away like this. You did nothing wrong and you have a desirable placement in the floating city. Don't do this."

Lessie shrugged. "Look, Phera. You're my best friend, you always have been, and going to the north is horrible, but going alone is even worse, and. . .I've wanted something more for a long time. Something I can't quite put my finger on, but this is an adventure, a true challenge. You're going to want someone who loves you there, on your side."

Tears filled my eyes and I kneeled beside her. The enormity of what I'd done and who it affected suddenly made sense to me. "Lessie, I can't let you do this. It's too much of a burden on me. I'm the one who's being sent away and punished. You can't—"

Lessie gave a tearful snort. "Don't cry, you'll make me join in too. Besides, they were going to send another mage anyway, a volunteer. If not me, it would be someone else. This isn't about you, Phera, it's bigger than that. The ice lords sent a request and the academy is beholden to fulfill it. I wanted you to hear it from me." She stood. "I have to pack. Apparently, we're leaving tomorrow at first light. Official papers are being drawn up and Mage Idelle, the historian, will accompany us as far as the outpost. From there, we're on our own."

Words failed me, so instead of protesting more, I leaned over and hugged her. Lessie was right—being alone on a new adventure, especially to the edges of the unknown lands, would be difficult. I wondered what the ice lords needed and what was so important that it was a matter of life and death. It was frightening how urgent their message sounded. Why would they change all stipulations, let down their guard and invite magic into their midst? This could go well, or might be the start of a war.

Lessie left me shortly after to pack and I was alone with my thoughts, which kept unraveling and twirling, going to dark and dangerous suspicions. On the one hand, I was grateful that Lessie was going with me. It was honorable and selfless of her to want to both assist me with my punishment and assist the ice lords. But the crypticness of her words made me wonder why. If everything was going well with her position, she would stay because she had a duty to the floating city first. I wondered if something had happened and she'd be willing to share with me.

On the other hand, I still felt responsible for her, and the fact that I was going as punishment lay a heavy burden on my shoulders. It was my fault, and she was suffering the consequences of my actions. I promised myself I'd be more careful in the future because the mages were correct—my actions had unintended consequences.

That night, I couldn't sleep. In the darkness, the vestiges of my nightmare lingered. In the academy, mages were taught to pay attention to dreams and the premonitions they might pertain to. Now, I understood the monster in my dream, ripping me out of my old life and bringing me somewhere new and unknown.

Mage Idelle came for me in the early hours, giving me time to dress and braid my curls before we were off, twisting through the long and airy passageways of the academy. I hadn't been outside in a month and I blinked in appreciation as we reached the rooftop, where the flight master readied three beasts.

Flying was the fastest way to get around Ethunia, and at each outpost were various ways to travel as quickly as possible. They involved travel by water, by land, or air. The beasts we were traveling on today were called Leviathans, a cross between a bird, a dragon, and a lizard. They were small and fast in the air, and what might be a three-week journey by land quickly turned into a three-day journey by air. The only downside with Leviathans was that they tired quickly because of their speed and had short lifespans. Breeding them was of the utmost importance, but there was concern that at the rate they were used, they'd become extinct. The animals were vicious, even muzzled, and strapping in for the ride was no easy feat.

But I lifted my face to the dew-damp day, tasting the moisture in the golden hues of sunshine on my tongue. My skin warmed and magic buzzed within, fighting to get out, held back, tamed by the bracelets. On the rooftop, I had a beautiful view of the Academy of Mages, a spiraling palace of light with manicured gardens and lawns stretching in all directions. Even the forests had paved paths, leaving the forest floor undisturbed and creating a harmonious coexistence between nature and humanity.

I bit back the bile that surged in my throat. Either way, whether I went to the dungeons or north to the realm of the ice lords, I'd be leaving this land for a significant amount of time, perhaps forever.

Suddenly, Mage Idelle—who had been silent since she came to collect me—yanked me to a stop and pulled me close. She smelled of parchment, and I knew her long fingers would be stained with ink. She had a passion for words, and under her tutelage, I'd learned the importance of archives and histories and how the actions of the past often informed the actions of the future. She had always been kind to me and generous with her time. Even though our private conversations had been few, they had been memorable, and I held her in the highest regard. Disappointing her stung as though I'd personally gone out of my way to slap her in the face.

"Phera," she whispered, holding my gaze intently. "The academy wasn't completely truthful with you. It is my advice that you abandon this quest to the northern countries. The ice lords haven't invited us into their midst before. We barely got them to sign the peace treaty and I have concerns. They have not been vetted. We don't know how savage they are, nor their customs or culture."

My head throbbed, but I refused to give in to speculation. Not now. "I understand your concerns, but it isn't the first time I've faced a challenge. Lessie is with me, and magic will protect us."

Mage Idelle's hard expression did not waver. "Perhaps, but the academy did not give you the full picture. You and Lessie will go as mage brides."

*Brides.* The word hummed in my mind and I blinked, not taking in the full meaning. As it sank in, my gaze tore across the rooftop. Was this the reason Lessie hadn't arrived yet?

"As in. . .we will be married. But why? Does Lessie know this?"

Mage Idelle sighed. "She does. I shared with her last night when I begged her to reconsider. She believes that one or both of you will be able to talk the ice lords out of such an arrangement, or at least the marriages will be in name only. She's not taking this seriously, but you should. This is part of the punishment."

I closed my eyes, my stomach sour. "We can't let Lessie come with us. She can't throw away her life like this."

"Running is reckless." Mage Idelle stepped back. "When we are faced with problems, we need to find a solution instead of running away or hiding from them."

My eyes narrowed. "You think that's what Lessie is doing?"

"It's only a hunch. Perhaps she will share the truth with you."

So something had happened at Lessie's posting in

the floating city. I wondered what was so bad that she'd choose a punishment over freedom. I didn't like it all, nor the way the academy had hidden the truth from me. A mage bride? That changed everything.

I was already mounted when Lessie appeared, dragging her bag behind her, long hair unbrushed as though she'd woken up, realized she was late, and dashed to the rooftop. She waved briefly before climbing aboard her own mount, and moments later, we were airborne.

I clutched the saddle, fingers wrapped across the reins. Flying was left to the skill of holding on, and the Leviathans were hypnotized. They only flew from one flight point to the other because of magic. Breaking their focus or attempting to control them was a crime. Only flight masters could control the Leviathans. The rest of us paid to ride. Occasionally, a beast went missing, but the magical trackers always allowed it to be tracked down and found, and strict record keeping noted who rode what beast at what times. Those who were riding when the beast went missing were fined and their flight privileges removed. It was a major inconvenience for mages who needed to travel quickly, and a risk rarely took.

In fact, many of the laws in Ethunia were to prevent crime and to preserve law and order, and peace. If everyone obeyed the rules, there would be harmony. Yet crime persisted, and this was why mages were needed and given an influential position of authority in almost every city.

Except the north. Which made me wonder. What kind of lawlessness abided in the land of the ice lords, and why did they request mage brides?

# Phera

Three days later, the Leviathans circled a tower with a flat rooftop. Cascading below it were rolling hills, dotted with stone homes. Low-lying rock walls marked the barriers between each home and the surrounding pasture land, free of anything taller than a few feet. To the north, the land sloped up to a glittery mountain perched on the edge of choppy waters which stretched as far as the eye could see. I eyed the frothy waves, midnight blues tipped with pale, foamy white, the color of old ice. A shiver went up my spine. I'd landed on the edge of the unknown lands where the barrier of civilization frayed, giving way to mysteries, monsters, and untold horrors. Rumor had it that those who lived in proximity to the unknown lands turned barbaric. It was likely why the ice lords were called savages. No one knew what they did to survive.

I dismounted, stretching my sore body. Three days of flying had taken its toll. I'd assumed that we'd stay at an inn during nightfall, but instead, we'd kept going, making a total of twelve stops. In my mind, it had seemed excessive, but there was an urgency in the letter, and I hadn't had more than a moment to say a few words to Lessie. I turned toward her, but Mage Idelle blocked my path.

Her fingers closed around my wrists as she whispered the magical words to set me free. The bracelets came loose with a tiny clicking sound and a roaring filled my ears. I squeezed my eyes shut as it raced around me, boiling, leaping, then settling, calming into an ocean of magic at my beck and call. I was free. Again. My gut reaction was to use magic instantly, but I sensed it would be stepping out of line. I didn't want to draw negative attention to myself because my ordeal was far from over.

Mage Idelle dropped the bracelets into a bag and thrust it into my hands. "Here, these are for you to give your husband on your wedding night, as a sign of trust. You are giving him the keys to your magic. A union between a mage and a non-mage is unique, and even though he lacks magic, it allows him to have power over you. If he ever has reason to fear you, he can suppress your magic."

My head buzzed, alive with the magic leaping inside of me, but I accepted the magical bracelets and tucked them into the wide pocket of my cloak. I had no intention of giving them to anyone, especially not my future husband. Now that I was free, I'd do everything in my power to ensure magic never got taken away from me again.

Mage Idelle squeezed my arm. "I'm going to speak with the flight master. Once the delegation from the city arrives, I will go."

My heart gave a pang. This was all happening so quickly.

With a nod, I joined Lessie, who was peering over the battlements. Most rooftops were built for battle, with stations for archers and swords and mages. This one was no different, except for one fact—it wasn't inside the city itself, but set apart from it. Should the ice lords need to defend themselves, the outpost outside of the city left them blind and vulnerable.

"Isn't it magnificent?" Lessie exclaimed.

"It is," I agreed, taking in the rich landscape. A wind blew in from the waters and I clutched my cloak around my throat. Air travel was cold but my cloak had been adequate, yet the briskness of the air out here made me want something warmer. We were only on the edges of late fall, and a heavy winter was yet to come, even though snow caps already graced the mountain ranges in the distance. "Lessie, do you know they want mage brides?"

She stiffened beside me, focus remaining on the landscape. "Aye, Mage Idelle warned me. It was duplicitous of the academy to keep that pertinent information from us. I don't understand why."

"Yet you didn't change your mind. You're still here."

"Yes."

I waited, giving her time to expand on her answer.

She didn't.

"What do you think?" I asked.

"It's an old tradition. The rites of marriage used to be how mages increased their magical prowess."

"I didn't study the old texts," I admitted.

"Ah, well, in ancient times, it was believed that a consummated marriage between a mage and a human—without magic—would increase the mage's magical abilities. But that thought is considered archaic and too close to dealings with blood magic."

My stomach clutched at the phrase *consummated marriage*, but I forced that thought away and focused on the curious fact that the ice lords believed in the old ways. But why would they want mages after all these years? Especially extremely powerful mages they could not control. Unless they already knew who their foe was and that magic was needed to defeat them. But we hadn't been called to war. Had we?

Lessie continued. "In some cases, the non-magical spouse gained something out of the marriage, whether it was power, magic, or something else the texts did not specify. There's no actual proof that it worked, which is why the practice was stopped."

"But mages rarely marry," I observed.

"No, but the academy has a reason for that. Marriage is distracting and seen as common. Settling down opens a mage up for vulnerabilities."

"That can't be the only reason. We are in a time of peace. Besides, non-mages marry and it doesn't make them vulnerable, nor are they seen as weak for welcoming love into their lives."

"I agree with you, Phera. I don't know why the stigma against mages and marriage remains. My only guess is because at one time, it was a requirement to access greater power. That was before the peace treaties and laws against corruption of magic were created."

All speculation aside, Lessie shared knowledge that was common in Ethunia. I wondered if the ice lords had archives about regulating mages and their power. It would be interesting to study what they thought of it and read the legends and tales stored in their archives.

"What's your plan then?" I asked. "Are you going to go along with the request and marry one of the ice lords?"

Lessie gave a quick glance over her shoulder to ensure no one was listening. Mage Idelle was on the other side of the rooftop where a man swallowed in furs was speaking with her. Still, Lessie kept her voice low. "I want to speak with them and understand the real reason they specifically requested mage brides. Perhaps they are ignorant of our ways in the southern lands. They might believe it is the only way to welcome mages into their midst and we can tell them the truth."

Somehow, I doubted savages would be interested in the truth, especially not from mages. "And if they don't understand and force us to go along with their plans?"

"There's always an option. A way out. We should help them, but perhaps we can do so before the ceremony. There might be a way out of here that doesn't involve flying."

I glanced back at the Leviathans, which had disappeared from sight to be fed and rested. It dawned on me that we were essentially trapped in the north, without a way out, unless we went on foot. The water blocked our retreat south, which meant going deeper into the ring of mountains and treading into the dark and dangerous unknown lands. Magic aside, it would be a terrifying ordeal.

"Just. . .whatever you decide to do, Lessie, keep talking to me. We're alone out here and it's—"

Lessie's hand landed on mine and she squeezed. "I know. At least we have each other."

"Ready?" Mage Idelle's sharp voice broke our conversation.

I didn't like the edge in her tone, a hint of discomfort. I always viewed her as calm and confident, fully in control of her emotions, but the oddity of the situation must be getting to her too. At least she had the option to leave.

We joined her in front of a trap door which stood open, stone stairs leading down into the tower.

"The delegation is downstairs, waiting for us," Mage Idelle explained. "I suspect I will be escorted back up here shortly to await my flight."

She grimaced, and I did not envy her three-day flight back to the academy. At least at each tower, we were given a meal and an hour to stretch our legs between flights. However, the hospitality in the north was severely lacking. We hadn't been offered any refreshments—in fact, no one had greeted us, aside from the surly flight master. It did not bode well for a beneficial working relationship. Nor did making assumptions and leaping to conclusions, so I attempted to bury my furtive thoughts.

The bottom floor of the tower opened into a wide room with arched windows without glass, letting in the generous light. I slipped off the last step, wishing I'd had more time to prepare. For once, I felt wholly inadequate, for indeed, a delegation had come to meet us. They simply hadn't taken the time to climb to the top of the tower.

Dozens of armed, muscled, bearded men filled the open space. They were all shapes and sizes, some with wild, unkempt hair, others neat and shaven. A mix of furs and leathers covered their hardened warrior bodies and my eyes took in the spears and shields leaning against the walls, the knives in belts, swords in sheaths, and axes, some with one blade, others with two. A group sat around a table, eating, drinking, and playing some kind of game with blades. Others stood near the door, weapons drawn, an alertness to their poses as though some grave menace would hurtle in from above or beyond the doors.

When we walked into the room, all conversation died away, and dozens of hard eyes fixed on us. I wished I had the ability to portal myself to a safe place, away from those intent eyes. I hadn't been nervous before, but even with magic surging behind my breastbone and tingling in my fingers, the desire to run was over- whelming.

Searching for a distraction, I noticed two women among the sea of men. One with bright-red hair rose from in front of a roaring fire and clasped her hands together, her green eyes rounding. The other stayed seated in a corner. A curved wood bow rested in her lap and slender fingers tapped her knee. It was her dress and the shape of her body that gave her away, because a curtain of long, black hair covered her face. So the term "ice warrior" encompassed both men and women.

Mage Idelle, having enough of the tension-filled silence, stepped forward. Her calm voice rang across the room. "Greetings, lords of the north. I am Mage Idelle, a representative from the Academy of Mages. I've come as escort to Mage Phera and Mage Lessie, who have volun- teered to come to your aid, as requested in this letter." She produced a scroll and held it up. "In accordance with the peace treaty, we have answered your request, and in exchange, ask that you treat the mages with the decorum and respect you would give to any city official."

A ripple went through those gathered at her last words. It was a silent ripple, but I sensed the change, the threat behind her words. I wished her words unsaid the moment they left her lips, because she would march upstairs and take a flight home while Lessie and I dealt with the fallout. But a display of confidence might be best against these hardened warriors, so keeping my shoulders back and head high, I searched the room, letting them know I wasn't afraid.

My gaze landed on one man, and, as ridiculous as it was, my heart skipped.

He stood by the door, one foot in, one out, as though his arrival was an afterthought. A knot of black hair rested on the top of his head and eyes the color of a foggy morning were deep set in his face. He wasn't scowling, nor was his expression pleasant. He gripped an axe with two curved blades on either side of the handle. A black and silver fur rested on his shoulders, but his arms were bare, displaying thick, corded muscles. He looked strong enough to lift a tree.

I'd seen men like him in the cities, men who prowled the night, searching for and dealing with trouble, but none had arrested my attention before. Not like this one. Decorum said I should look away, not stare boldly at such a man, but he shifted, moving fully inside.

Light fell on his black hair and gave me a better view of his bearded face. He was younger than I'd first thought, but then he lifted his head and those steely gray eyes met mine. They were hard, unflinching, holding a challenge.

Magic sang in my fingertips, and it took all I had to hold back from answering his challenge.

It took me a moment before I realized someone else was speaking, and I forced myself to look away, my ears burning as though they'd been touched by a hot poker.

# Phera

"Well met," a deep, authoritative voice boomed.

The ice lords stood back as a giant of a man moved toward us. I shrank into myself, watching how he was at least a head and shoulder taller than any man in the room, and the looks they all gave him were a combination of admiration and respect.

He held out a meaty hand as he approached. "Lady Phera, Lady Lessie, I am Lord Edwin. Welcome to our lands. We are honored you have chosen to grace us with your presence."

I shook his beefy hand, words thick in my throat. At least some of the ice lords had manners, but while the greeting sounded humble and meaningful, it stank of a false facade. I wondered if he was the one who'd sent for us, and whether it was his idea to request mage brides.

"We are here to assist you in any way that we can," Lessie said, parroting the words we'd memorized during our years at the academy. At least the proper decorum hadn't forsaken her. But Lessie had always excelled under pressure. "We are eager to learn more about why our presence was requested. Shall we speak of these grave matters now?"

Lord Edwin clasped his hands together and stepped back. "No need. There will be time later. You must be famished from your journey. I hear it's a three-day flight by bird, no rest."

A Leviathan wasn't what I'd call a bird, but no matter—he was correct. Weariness sank into my bones, but apprehension kept me wide awake. What would happen to us?

"My men will escort you to Eyre Heights. Mage Idelle, you'll be leaving us soon. Have a meal and rest for a bit before you leave. I will sit here with you to discuss the peace accords."

So she had been right. Although Lord Edwin did not explicitly tell her to leave, his words held the same meaning. She was unwanted.

"I am at your service." Mage Idelle nodded her head. "But I would see my mages settled."

"Ah, to those matters." Lord Edwin turned and waved his hand. "Lord Rhyme, Lord Isak."

Two of the fur-clad warriors approached. One had thick red hair that stuck up from his head as though it refused to lie flat. He had a short, trim beard and wore furs and insignia depicting an axe cleaving a horn in half. I wondered what it meant as I turned my attention to the other man, steeling myself as I realized it was the one I'd made eye contact with earlier.

Those gray eyes lingered on me again, and I reminded myself that Lessie and I were oddities in their region. We should expect an untoward amount of attention given our status. But there was something hypnotic, almost magnetic, about him.

Faintly, I heard Lord Edwin make introductions. "Lord Rhyme, please escort Lady Phera, your future bride, and Lord Isak, please escort Lady Lessie, your future bride, to Eyre Heights."

Those words were for my and Lessie's benefit. In one blow, he'd introduced us to our future husbands and sent us away from Mage Idelle. It took all my strength to whirl back to her and squeeze her hand. "Thank you," I managed before Lord Edwin took her elbow and escorted her to one of the recently vacated tables.

"Dismissed!" he roared with all the luster of a true savage.

I wasn't even out of the room before I disliked that man.

The tower emptied quickly. While a few of the warriors settled near the door, the rest marched out in a line as though they were going to battle.

I took a step and my future husband was right there, towering above me, his stony expression unreadable. Determined not be intimidated, I lifted my chin to look him full in the face. Up close, those gray eyes sparked with intensity, and I noticed the faint scar on the side of one cheek. The axe hadn't left his hand either, and it was frighteningly close. Was he waiting for me to unleash my magic so that he could lop off my head?

"Lord Rhyme." His title and name were the only words that would escape my lips.

"Lady Phera," he echoed, offering his arm.

I took it, my fingers moving across warm skin, the hair on his arm surprisingly soft. Still, a slew of terrible thoughts filled my mind. Unlike Lessie, I was under no false pretenses that we'd be able to avoid the arranged marriages. But I needed to figure out a way to make this work, otherwise I was sentencing myself to a hellish life. Lord Rhyme's tension filled-silence did not help, and I could think of no words to say to him.

I licked my dry lips, a lump forming in my throat. This wasn't how I wanted to meet him, in clothes I'd worn the past three days, without the chance to bathe or re-braid my windblown hair. Fatigue settled in, and despite my anxiety, a deep hunger gnawed at the pit of my belly. A full night of sleep—not on the back of a Leviathan—and a bath would quicken my wits.

We'd taken no more than a few steps outside when a female voice rang out behind us. "Oh, enough with the formalities. Let me escort them."

Lord Rhyme dropped his arm and pivoted as a redheaded woman fell into step beside me. "I'm Bonnie," she announced, giving first me, then Lessie a cheeky grin. She waved her hand at Lord Rhyme and Lord Isak. "Go on ahead. I'll take care of them and return them to you in due time."

Those gray eyes found mine, and he gave me a nod. A short-lived relief settled into me as he took the lead and we followed, only a few paces behind. Warriors surrounded us on all sides as we navigated the rocky path toward the mountain.

"My apologies," Bonnie said, glancing from me to Lessie. "The lords of Eyre Heights are not used to dealings with mages. The show of bravery was so you wouldn't see how frightened they are of you." She gave a harsh laugh.

Lessie raised an eyebrow. "Frightened? Why would they call on us if they are frightened of our magic?"

"I joke," Bonnie said with a shrug. "Truth is, no one from the southern lands have visited us, and we're rusty with our welcoming skills. You must be exhausted from your journey."

"Try three days of flying without rest. You'd be exhausted too," Lessie murmured.

I glanced at her, sensing that her good behavior was fading into irritation. "We could use a bath, a change of clothes, and a meal," I said. "Do you know what the plan is for our time here?"

"Impressive. You're all business, aren't you?"

"I heard it was a matter of life and death," I told her.

"Everything is a matter of life and death here," Bonnie groused. "You've met the lords and the warriors." She rattled off the names of the rest of the delegation. "Once we reach Eyre Heights, I'll take you to the pools where you can bathe, eat, and then rest. We haven't planned anything else until tomorrow. You'll meet with the lords to discuss the reason you're here, and you'll have seven days to settle in before the ceremony."

"The marriage ceremony?" Lessie interrupted.

"Aye," Bonnie said.

A numbness settled over me and I couldn't bring myself to say anything else, even though my silence made me appear stiff and rude. Instead, I turned my attention to our surroundings.

We followed the slope down to the road that led up to a jagged mountainside. Towers jutted from the cliffs, giving me an understanding of the name of their home. Eyre Heights—a home in the mountainside. However, the rolling hills that led down to the sea boasted of wide green pastures and smaller homes that dotted the area. Farmland?

While no snow covered the ground, a damp chill that smelled of snow hung in the air. It seldom snowed in the southern lands, but when it did, the weather turned peculiar. I recalled the feel of it on my skin, cold kisses that melted, making my magic come alive with the atmosphere.

Despite my predicament, I could appreciate the stark beauty of the land—the hues of blue that stretched across the sky, the ripple of the sea reflecting the golden rays of sunlight, and the way beads of water hung on the grass and shrubs like jewels. It was peaceful, with a few animals grazing in the pasture land, fishers by the sea, and a mountainous retreat for safety. There was still the oddity of the tower, the outpost by itself, with no protection.

By the time we reached the city entrance, I was out of breath. Light poured in from the hollowed-out mountain, a gentle current of cool air rippling through the city, yet nothing like the buffing wind that left me chilled through and through.

In the distance, jagged stairs led up to the heights, and pointed watch towers appeared. On either side of the twisting road, signs swung in the gentle breeze and a hubbub of voices swelled. There were shops with signs above them, homes, and an endless surge of people, much like the bustling cities in the south.

I'd misjudged the place.

The quaint farmlands were nothing but a decoy to hide the true wealth of the city. I came to a stand still, my head tilted back as I took in Eyre Heights, and suddenly, I understood. Lord Edwin was protecting his people and his land by keeping the outpost on the outskirts. Mage Idelle would never see the remarkable city, nor be able to return to the southern lands and discuss what she'd seen. It was all intentional.

A cold shiver went down my back and I attempted to make eye contact with Lessie, but Bonnie blocked my view. Regardless, I had a hunch that something was not right here.

The bath was a natural hot spring in the bowels of the mountain. Winding stone stairs led down into the cave-like structure where the waters rippled dark and murky. Light came from the glistening walls and an opening high above. I expected the air to be chilling, but the steam rising from the pool was enough to keep warm.

I stripped out of my clothes and slipped into the pool while Lessie conservatively dipped her finger in the water. She looked pained. I guessed she disliked the inky blackness—the pools in the academy were transparent—and the way the water wormed away into the walls, hiding its source. But I had another reason for entering the pool so quickly. My magic was attuned to water, and sure enough, a warm glow surrounded me and magic oozed out of my fingertips.

Something between a sigh and a cry tore out of my lips. The murky darkness faded and motes of light filled the cavern, showing off the way the water had eroded it. The glitter of gold drew my attention to the bottom of the pool and I gaped in astonishment, tracking the glitter all the way up the sides of the cavern to the top where light poured in.

So that was the secret of the ice lords. They lived in a mountain with a vein of gold in its heart. How much did they mine from here? How wealthy were they?

Lessie must have seen, too, because she made a

small sound in her throat. When I faced her, she quickly splashed water on her face. "Phera," she whispered.

I glanced around the cave. We were seemingly alone. Bonnie had left to find us clothes and food. I appreciated her leaving us because I couldn't get a good read on her. Was she friendly or just attempting to make light of an awkward situation?

"What do you think?" I asked, moving to the side to pick up a bar of soap. It smelled like eucalyptus and wild roses.

Lessie slipped into the water, her expression careful. She worked up a lather before responding. "Seven days. We have to work quickly."

# Phera

Light bloomed across my face and I peeked one eye open to blush rays tinged with orange. I was lying face down in a delightful pile of furs. I couldn't recall ever being so comfortable in my life and I snuggled in deeper, inhaling the peace and warmth and comfort that surrounded me. When was the last time I'd felt so relaxed?

Suddenly, I jerked upward, memories crashing back into my mind. Lessie and I were in the north in the mountain called Eyre Heights. After bathing and eating, we'd been determined to speak with the ice lords. After all, we had seven days before the marriage ceremony and we didn't have a moment to lose. Except I'd slept. The last I recalled was that redheaded woman, Bonnie, escorting us to our chambers.

Furs tumbled off the bed as I stood, squinting against the light. I was alone in a small room, but it was bright and airy, a sharp contrast to the prison cell. Light shone in from a floor-to-ceiling window situated directly across from the bed. To one side of the window, an open chest set against the wall, with clothes and furs overflowing from it.

I hadn't been able to bring any of my belongings with me. When the mages discovered what I'd done, they'd instantly suppressed my magic and transported me to the Academy of Mages. I imagined at some point my luxurious chambers in the palace were given to the mage who took my place. The memory burned, and I forced it away. I'd never see that place again. I was in the north, on the edges of the unknown lands, and needed to focus on the task at hand.

Going to the chest, I dressed quickly, assuming all the clothes belonged to me. They were feminine, although aside from the dresses and furs, there was also a jerkin and pants, boots, and a belt. The garb of a hunter. Would I be hunting? I supposed anything was possible, yet I chose the dress and slipped my feet into a pair of moccasins. The clothing was slightly big, but it was warm. When I turned around to find a looking glass, I discovered that there were two doors leading out of the room. Curious.

Choosing one at random, I pressed my palm against it and closed my eyes. My magic didn't allow me to see through walls or doors, but I could detect body heat and sometimes potent emotion. Nothing came from the other side, and so I opened the door.

I expected to find a washroom or a closet, but not an entire room. Its layout was similar to mine with access to the same white-stoned balcony. The room was clearly lived in, embers dying in a fireplace that sat against one wall, thick carpets covering the floor, and a bed shrouded in brown and black furs. There were boots and clothing and swords, and knives, axes, and shields lined one wall. The wall of a warrior. I gawked at it, my chest going tight as I took in the antlers jutting from a wall. This was a man's room. Lord Rhyme's room?

It made sense. It was adjoined to mine. Separate rooms. Separate beds. I had seven days to escape all this, yet I lingered.

Mages didn't marry, but part of me wondered if it would be so terrible to live within a sacred boundary of trust and love and companionship. It felt wrong for something so essential to be off limits to mages because of magic. Like Lessie and I had discussed, the old ways required a union between a mage and a non-magical human. What had changed?

A knock came from the other door, startling me. I

shut the door to Lord Rhyme's room and ran my fingers through my loose curls. Was Lessie at the door? It was full daylight and time to get to work. I hastened toward it and threw it open, words of relief forming on my lips, until I saw who stood on the other side.

Lord Rhyme leaned against the doorframe, his bulk making it impossible to see beyond him. My eyes lingered on his loose jerkin and his dark hair pulled partially back from his face into a bun, the rest of it hanging loosely around his shoulders. His gray eyes widened slightly as his gaze roamed over me. "Lady Phera, I hoped we might have a word."

I arched an eyebrow, struggling to regain my tongue. This was my second meeting with him, and this time, I wouldn't botch it, like the first one. "Please, call me Phera."

His expression softened. "Only if you call me Rhyme."

*Ah, so he can relax.* "Rhyme. It's a good name."

"So is Phera."

My lips turned up in relief. Was this the same stoic warrior I'd met yesterday? "I had no choice in it, but I thank you."

"Did you have a choice in coming here?"

I held his gaze, surprised at the question. "It was my choice," I said flatly. It was the truth, yet there was much more behind those words. Pushing away the encroaching edges of guilt, I kept my head high. "Speaking of, shall we discuss why I'm here?"

Rhyme winced and stepped away from the door. "Aye."

I followed him into a spacious bower, where my feet sank into a carpet of furs. A window seat overlooked the same view as the balcony in my room. I wanted to gain a better sense of my surroundings, but a curling white mist blocked the view. Orange flames leaped in a stone fireplace and stacks of wood sat beside it. In front of it, to one side, was a table with a generous heaping of food and a pile of books and scrolls. Did those belong to Rhyme? He appeared more warrior and less studious, but I knew nothing about him. Assumptions would only lead to trouble. To the other side was a couch, and beyond it, shelving with various items and a couple of chests.

Rhyme gestured to the table. "I assumed you'd be hungry and I wasn't sure what you'd like. . ." He trailed off, and my heart warmed at his thoughtfulness.

"I'm not picky," I said, striding across the room to take a seat, suddenly aware of how alone we were together.

Rhyme sat down across from me and rested his elbows on the table. "Help yourself. I already ate."

I felt self-conscious eating while he watched me, so I poured a glass of water while I studied the bounty. There was jam, poached eggs, sausage, bread, and cheese. While I filled my plate, Rhyme poured himself a warm brew that smelled slightly bitter. I'd heard that northern men liked their beer, but it didn't appear like ale.

I picked up a fat sausage and wrapped it between bread and cheese. "These are your chambers?"

Rhyme frowned and took a sip of his odd brew. "Our chambers."

I took a bite of sausage and immediately repressed the groan of satisfaction that rose on my lips. The food here was delectable. I snuck another glance at Rhyme, who was strangely quiet for someone who wanted to talk. I couldn't get a good read on him.

As I chewed, I realized I had to set the expectations for our working relationship. I had to show him how I expect to be treated. I'd been led to believe that something terrible was happening here and I couldn't help unless he opened up and talked to me. In the Academy of Mages, I had studied about inspiring trust in others and how to gain it. It often started by opening oneself up and being vulnerable. Which meant I had to talk first.

Tucking my curls behind one ear, I filched a napkin from the table and wiped off my fingers. "It's uncommon for mages to be requested in the north, especially mage brides. Nor is it a practice in the southern lands, but I understand you have a dire need. I want to hear what it is, to understand how I can help."

Now I had his attention. "You're direct, aren't you?"

I pressed my lips together, waiting.

Rolling his shoulders back, he sighed. "Not everyone agreed with requesting mages to assist with the. . .situation here. But as a bride, you will be part of the clan. You will have the respect of the people and my protection."

*His* protection. "My magic will not be enough protection?"

A muscle in his jaw jumped. "No. My people keep to the old ways. We fight with our bare hands, with weapons, not with words and spells."

I bristled at the insult and opened my mouth, ready to retort, but Rhyme held up his hand. "This is a difficult situation. It has political implications, and if not resolved by the next full moon, the future of my entire clan will be in question. Does the weightiness of this situation bother you?"

Fighting to stay calm, I shook my head. "It is expected. One would not call on a mage unless the circumstances were dire. As I understand it, that has never happened in the many lifetimes of the Academy of Mages. Why?"

Rhyme studied me silently. "I would like our relationship to be built on a foundation of trust and honesty. That is most important to me."

I squeezed my hands together to keep from flinching. Honesty would mean telling him about my past and the reason I was in Eyre Heights. I recalled the way Mage Idelle had pressed the magical suppression bracelets into my hands, giving me the choice to tell Rhyme about them. . .or not. . .

Sitting up straighter, I tucked my hands into my lap, keeping my tone even. "What are you asking of me?"

"My people, myself included, know little about magic. I'm aware that not all mages have the same abilities, but often, they are strengthened during a. . .union."

A fluttering behind my breastbone made me shift in astonishment. How did he know *that* fact? He must have done his research on the history of mages. It was a fact alluded to, but rarely discussed, how mages might find their magic more potent after a marriage, more specifically after consummating a marriage. So, this was not to be a marriage in name only. An image of him lowering his body over mine, hot lips tracing lines over my skin, flashed through my vision.

My lips fell open. "It's true," I gasped. "In some instances."

Rhyme set his elbows on the table and made a tent

with his hands. "What kind of magical abilities do you have?"

The question was put forth so bluntly it took me a moment to collect my thoughts. One was rarely asked for a list of abilities.

"My magic has an affinity for water. I can draw it from the air and use it as light or form it into a weapon. I also have heightened senses. I can touch something and sense the echo from it, usually an emotion."

Rhyme listened without movement and I wondered if he understood. My chest went tight as I remembered when they found me. It was the only time I'd attempted to defend my actions. I was panicked, frightened, and I started talking, quickly, overexplaining myself. Looking back, I wondered if my tongue had sealed my guilt more than my actions.

"People haven't always understood your magic, have they?" Rhyme asked.

My eyes snapped to his and my hands trembled. How much did he know?

"Not always." I shifted my focus to the fire. "Mages haven't always been understood, nor has magic, hence the rise of the academy, to control magic in their own way."

"Everything shouldn't be controlled," Rhyme mused.

I dared myself to study him and sensed empathy in his gaze. "What happened?" I asked, steering the conversation back to the reason I was there.

Rhyme leaned forward, his shadow crossing over mine. It was the pain in his voice—not his proximity— that left me shivering. "We are being haunted by a menace. It comes at night, using neither doors nor walls. It moves as if invisible and it steals people—women, mostly. A few young lads have gone missing, but more recently, it's just the women. We've combed the mountainside, searching for them all, to no avail. At first, we thought they were running away, but it made little sense. Mothers left their young behind, a babe sleeping by the fire, a toddler in the wood. Some vanished while bringing in the animals and left the gates open, allowing wolves to get in." Rhyme sighed and scrubbed a hand over his face. "We went hunting and retraced all the disappearances. It was Lord Isak who found an oddity, strange symbols left behind with every disappearance. That's when we knew it was too much for us and we needed help of a magical kind." Rhyme reached for a scroll and unrolled it, displaying runic symbols. "These two runes were left on the floor of every home where someone went missing."

I stared at the runes on the scroll and a slow, sick feeling spread through my gut. Swallowing hard, I bowed my head so he wouldn't see my reaction. Blindly, I reached for the scroll and ran my fingers over the parchment, waiting for the sensation to rush through me. But my magic didn't speak to me—fear did.

The day I'd disobeyed the rules of the academy and used blood magic for my own purposes was also the day I saw runes, similar to these, for the first time.

There was a catch in my voice when I finally spoke, dizzy from what I was seeing. "How long has this been going on?"

"On and off for months," Rhyme said. "You know something? You believe you can help?"

"I can help," I confirmed, my mind racing. "I need to study these. Do you have an archive? Or library? I also need the counsel of Mage Lessie."

"I will escort you there myself," Rhyme said.

And then his hand came down over mine, firm and warm. I jerked my head up and my heart turned over. I sensed something else from him, an emotion I couldn't name. All the same, a sudden knowing came over me.

I was in trouble.

# Phera

The archives were underground, beneath a layer of rock, but when Rhyme pushed open the heavy doors, sunshine welcomed us. We stepped into a hall of muted silence where stone shelves towered above us. I wasn't sure what I expected, great tomes perhaps, but not rounded tubes protecting scrolls, laid across the shelves. The practice of scroll-writing felt as archaic as the aura of the place.

A narrow window in the back of the room over-looked the waters with craggy rocks, warning of what would happen if one fell. It was wild and beautiful, and an ache began in my chest. I turned to Rhyme, who had been quiet as he led me there. A man of few words. I could come to appreciate that.

"Thank you." My fingers brushed across his arm, the

contact incidental, yet a zing shuddered through my veins.

Rhyme pointed across to the room to where a figure stood by the window. Lessie.

She turned at the intrusion and her face brightened. "Phera." She hastened toward us, stopping to curtsy. "Lord Rhyme."

He turned to me. "I have some business to attend to. Stay here until myself, Lord Isak, or Lady Bonnie comes for you." Without waiting for a response, he pivoted and strode away.

The doors to the archives shut with a muted thud and I watched them, an inkling of discomfort dancing up my spine. *Stay here.*

Lessie poked my side. "I am glad to see you, Phera."

I glanced around the hall. "Are we alone here?"

She shrugged. "The archivist left a few moments before you arrived. I could tell he wasn't keen on leaving me alone in here and there's something uncanny about this place. It's as though the scrolls are watching, listening."

I knew what she meant as I shivered even though it wasn't cold in the room. "Perhaps it's simply the weight of the legends that are stored here. I imagine there are many secrets. Tell me, what did you discover while I was sleeping? Have you done any work?"

Lessie led me to a table where books and scrolls were rolled out. "I've had a headache and it's difficult to concentrate. It's hard to remember last night." Lessie scrunched up her nose. "Do you think we were drugged?"

I sat down, planting my feet firmly on the ground, trying to recall the night before. "I don't think so, Lessie. We flew for three days without rest. Finally having a chance to clean ourselves and eat led to the exhaustion, not being drugged."

Lessie drummed her fingers on the table. "Well, regardless, we have to be careful here. They know nothing about mages and magic, and we only have seven days to persuade them against binding us in holy matrimony."

I studied Lessie, wondering if my behavior was as odd as hers. It was wise to keep our own counsel, but we were here to work, not speculate. Unrolling the scroll, I showed her the runes. "Rhyme told me about the disappearances and the runes left in place. What do you make of these?"

Lessie barely looked at the runes. "I spoke with Lord Isak, and he told me the same. It sounds like women want to escape this place. What if they are all in on a prank? A joke?"

I weighed the words, wondering if I'd missed something. "It could be possible. Rhyme said at first, they assumed the women were running away. But the runes left behind made them reconsider."

"Rhyme. You call him by his first name." A smile played about her lips. "Did you have an intimate conversation with him?"

My blood went cold. I knew Lessie was teasing me, yet she voiced what I refused to consider in the privacy of my own thoughts. "We have to work together, Lessie. This is my punishment. You don't have to be here. If you took a flight south, they'd welcome you back."

Lessie reached across the table and squeezed my hand. "You're right, Phera. I'm out of sorts today, and grumpy. I just get the feeling that something isn't right."

"Because something *isn't* right," I agreed.

Lessie chewed her lower lip. "Can I be honest with you?"

*Was she finally going to reveal her secret?*

"I like him." Lessie sighed. "I expected to loathe him and. . .he's not what I thought. We had breakfast together this morning and. . .I like him. Time will tell if it changes, but he's reasonable. He listens when I speak, and he's not afraid of the idea of mages and magic. It's uncanny. I've never felt like this before, especially not in the floating city where I had to fight every day just to prove myself. You are probably wondering why I left and chose to endure your punishment with you. You must think I'm crazy."

"I am curious," I said, the runes forgotten.

"I was tired of fighting, of not being able to use my skills. The people in the floating city weren't kind. They belittled me because I was stepping into a position that had been long held. Lord Fry, you recall him? He had such a hold on that city. Even though he died and I took his place, the people acted as though it was *my* fault, as if I'd done the unforgiveable. They didn't trust me. They invented mischief, pranks to get me work and use magic for no reason. I was. . .belittled and made fun of. When I requested another placement, it was denied. . .but going with you to the edges of the unknown lands, well, it was an unforeseen gift. I'm aware that it might be the same here, but. . ."

"Lessie, I'm sorry. I had no idea. Why didn't you write to me?"

"How could I? I didn't know who to trust. I was watched. I had no privacy I. . .I can see how my feelings are making me misjudge this situation. Phera, you have a good head on your shoulders. You should take the lead here."

I studied her. "And when you say you *like* him, do you mean Lord Isak?"

"I'm not sure. I don't trust my judgment."

I rolled the scroll back up, watching her. "But what does that mean, Lessie? Yesterday, we made a plan."

"We were delirious from travel. Phera, I'm so tired of fighting. What if this is the place?"

"You just said you have a bad feeling about this place."

"I do, and yes, it's odd, dangerous," Lessie sputtered. She hung her head for a moment, gathering her chaotic thoughts. "All I'm saying is that we need to be careful and base our actions on facts, not emotion. I'm telling you this because I'm making decisions based on emotion and I don't feel normal. My betrothed is enticing, this place feels heavy, and we need to discover why the women are disappearing. But I don't want to do all of that. I want to rediscover my magic, find out if Lord Isak and I will be a good match, and to determine if we will eventually be safe here or if we need to run. Seven days is too much to do all of it."

In the past, I'd always appreciated Lessie's straightforward honesty, but this was too much. My frustration mounted, even though I tried to taper it down, gesticulating with my hands. "Then we make a plan. We divide and conquer. But first, we need to understand what is happening here. We heard from the ice lords, but we need first-hand witnesses."

Lessie straightened up. "What about Bonnie? Perhaps she can be of assistance."

"Did I hear my name?"

I spun, almost rising to my feet as Bonnie shut the doors behind her. Her sudden appearance was uncanny, as though she'd heard us speaking about her, but it wasn't possible. Not from that distance. Lessie and I had purposefully kept our voices low.

"Lady Bonnie, will you join us?" I asked, making room for her at the table.

Today, she wore her red hair in two long braids, along with pants and a jerkin. Belted around her waist was a sword and some knives, and my gaze lingered on those. Did she expect to be attacked inside? Or was it merely from habit?

Bonnie sat sideways on the bench, facing me, and leaned an elbow on the table. "Did you find anything?"

"I assume you're aware of what's going on," I started. "Do you have any connection with the women who disappeared? What can you tell us?"

Bonnie's face crumbled. "It stole my sister. I hate sitting here in the mountain, helpless. If it can get us in here, it can get us anywhere. I'm a warrior. I know how to fight, but how can I fight something I can't see or hear coming?"

"Were you there when it happened?"

She nodded. "It happened a few weeks ago in the farmlands close to the great sea. During the winter, everyone moves into the mountain. It's warmer, safer, and we bring all the animals too. But during the late spring, summer, and fall, before the first snowfall, we live in the lowlands. It's feral, but beautiful. No one understands how we can live on the edges of the unknown lands, and while it has its dangers, it has its freedom and beauty. But now one of the dangers has come to our doorstep, and we don't understand it."

Swiping at her face, Bonnie went on. "I was bringing in the sheep. They are ridiculous animals, you know, so stupid and difficult to corral. Eloise was inside with her wee babe, putting him down to sleep so she could make dinner. I was supposed to be helping her. She'd had a hard time, and I knew she didn't want her husband's mother to come live with them. Lord Landis is strict but fair and he didn't want to overwork his wife, knowing the babe was hard on her and all. I wanted to stay longer, but I'm no farmer or housewife. I'm a hunter, a warrior. That's the life I choose. I should have been inside helping her, but those damn sheep... And then I heard crying. When I ran inside, she was gone and nothing but those runes were there." She stabbed a finger down on the scroll with a viciousness that almost ripped it.

I stared at the runes, an idea forming. "Are the runes still there?"

"Where?"

"In the house where your sister disappeared. Are they still there?"

"Yes, why?"

I stood. "I need to see them."

# Phera

Shortly, we were on our way, escorted by Lord Rhyme, Lord Isak, and Bonnie. She fell into step with me, head held high, but the way her eyes shifted back and forth indicated her nervousness.

Our small party wound its way out of the layers of the mountain haven. This time, I tried to take note of anything unusual, but it was difficult in a place that was completely foreign to me.

People paused their work to watch us, no doubt disturbed at catching sight of the mages. The castle perched at the very back of the mountain, with cliffs overlooking the sea. Shops lined either side of the road—a tavern, a tailor, a blacksmith. A jeweler. I let my gaze linger, recalling the hot steam bath, the natural pool, and the gold that lined the bottom.

Eyre Heights had signed the peace treaty, but no mages were allowed there. Was it because of their wealth? Were they afraid the southern lands would abuse it? If so, the outpost being on the outskirts of the land made sense. If mages appeared in their land, it gave the ice people a chance to prevent them from seeing anything of importance—like Mage Idelle, who likely still believed that the northern lands were quaint, dangerous, and filled with savage warriors. It was the same sense I got from my quick arrival, but dwelling inside the mountain was changing my perspective.

And so was Rhyme. He offered me his arm and I held on to it as we stepped outside. A sharp wind blew, making me grateful for my furs and we followed a dirt path downhill between swelling hills and gray stones rising out of the ground. Despite being late fall, the grass was still a bright, emerald green, although it was short in some places, an indication of grazing herds. But my gaze was riveted to the water.

It swelled, a body with hues of blue, waves rolling and coasting, sometimes lapping at the shore, sometimes swelling in the distance. To the right of me, sky and sea stretched as far as the eye could see, and to the left was more land; behind, mountains.

"It's beautiful," I said, my breath puffing out like the breath of a Leviathan.

"How does it compare to the southern lands of the known world?" Rhyme asked.

"I don't think there is a comparison," I told him. "The southern lands are more built up. Nature is there, but it's been cultivated into carefully controlled gardens and forests. It's symmetrical and carries a beauty of its own, but out here, it's wild and unpredictable."

"Because we are on the edges of the unknown world," Rhyme said. "Unknown and unexplored."

Curiosity about his place in Eyre Heights urged my next question. "You're a warrior. Have you traveled far from the mountain?"

"You're asking if I've ventured into the unknown lands. I am a warrior, and a hunter. I've been over mountains and through thick forests. It's wild, untamable, and compelling."

Those words revealed more of him than our earlier conversion. "You like the wildness of it."

"I like a challenge," he confirmed.

"Me too. That's why I wanted to become a mage."

"You make it sound like you had a choice, as though the magic didn't choose you."

"I was twelve when I discovered the inklings of magic, fifteen when the mages came for me, and when I was eighteen, I joined the Academy of Mages and studied there for four years, learning how to control magic and the rules set forth by the governing body of mages. Magic chose me but I also wanted it. I wanted the life of a mage." I trailed off, buried memories rising to the forefront of my mind.

Once I graduated from the academy, I was assigned a placement, as every mage was. Usually, a group of no more than three were placed in each city and worked with the governors of that land to resolve disputes and protect the citizens from the blight of the unknown lands. I'd been on a bay, a place where I could use my water magic, for the city was rife with underground markets and illegal trade. The group of mages I worked with was tasked with finding the leader of the illegal trade market and bring him to justice. I'd found him. I'd brought him to justice. And that had been my downfall.

"You *wanted* the life of a mage? If that's what you still want, what brought you here?"

Punishment. Plain and simple. But I dodged the question. "I like a challenge."

"Perhaps you've met your match with these odd disappearances," Rhyme sighed. "At times, it seems supernatural."

I didn't respond to his speculation, because there was always a logical reason for what might appear unexplainable, and it was my task to find it.

"Here," Lord Isak called.

We paused in front of a small house with a thatched roof. A rock wall stretched behind it and we turned off the path into the yard.

Bonnie turned her back to it. "I'll keep watch out here," she said, a catch in her voice.

I turned to Lessie. "Are you coming in?"

Lessie's magic differed from mine, and I wasn't sure what she might find inside. She used her magic for protection and defense, while I used mine to be proactive. We made a good team together, and once again, I was grateful she'd decided to come with me.

"I'm going to inspect outside. I'll be in shortly," she countered.

I nodded while Rhyme forced open the door. The windows had been shuttered and I joined him in the darkness, the stale quiet of the room wrapping around me. There was an odor to it I couldn't put my finger on— not exactly a musty smell but something else, almost animal-like.

Rhyme left the door open as he moved further into the hut, allowing the light to shine in. It was a simple layout, a main room, a small pantry, and a curtain pulled across a section with a bed. A thin layer of dust covered the floor, and I sensed a presence. But that wasn't quite it.

I strode to the middle of the room. The furniture

had been pushed against the walls, leaving a clear path. There were no footprints other than mine, and I closed my eyes, letting myself feel the vestigial emotions. The frayed edges of tragedy still lingered there, making my throat close. Something horrible had happened there and goosebumps pebbled on my arms, despite the layers of fur I wore.

Closing my eyes, I let the riot of magic twirling inside settle to a steady current and picked out what irritated me most about the home.

It was in front of the fireplace.

My eyes blinked open in a flash and I stepped through the dust and crouched. The dust didn't quite cover it. I brushed my fingers over it impatiently, revealing the runes. There were two of them, just like on the scroll. The lines were identical, as if they had been traced, and I appreciated the concentration. But seeing the real thing sent alarms through me. Stretching out my fingers, I placed my palm flat against the runes and allowed my magic to attune to them. A vision swirled and I yanked my hand back. Visions? That had never happened before, only vague sensations.

I glanced over my shoulder to see Rhyme watching me, eyes dark. "Anything?"

The desperation was clear in his tone and I wanted to please him, wanted to give him something to help ease the burden of the unknown. "A little," I said. "I just need a few more minutes."

I turned back to the runes, flattened my palm, and closed my eyes. A jolt went through me and an ice-cold sensation crept up my arm. I was somewhere dark. Cold. An overpowering feral scent hung in the air, twisted with the burned char of fire and flesh.

A deep voice bellowed, and a hulking horned monster stomped into view. It was a combination of a giant and a beast, yet walked on two legs like a man. Goat-like hooves left deep impressions in the snow and it reared its horned head back and roared, displaying a furry maw, a snake-like thick tongue, and curved fangs. It froze, mid-roar as though something had disturbed it, and then pivoted toward me. Bloodshot golden eyes stared at me as though it were not a vision at all and the beast could truly see me. Then it lunged.

I yanked my hand away with a cry, reeling from what I'd seen. It had never happened before. It had never felt so visceral and real, as though what was out there had seen me, and knew I was on its trail.

"Phera." Rhyme's voice was steady, even, and his hand on my shoulder a comfort.

I stood. "I need ink and quill. I want to draw what I've seen."

# Phera

I ran my fingers down the papery edges of a scroll, tracing the lines there. The ink was raised, slightly uneven from being written, then dusted with powder while it dried. It was a sign of its age, for in this era, ink was mixed to dry quickly. It also had a smell to it, a hint of sweet sap mixed with the scent of wood and damp earth.

After the discovery of runes and my strange vision, Lessie had begged a headache and gone to lie down while I sought answers. The two runes I'd found in the hut were burned into my mind, as was the monster. I'd asked for ink and paper, and, to my surprise, Bonnie produced parchment and watercolors. Using a stick, I sketched the monster I'd seen, but when I presented the drawing to Rhyme, he didn't appear surprised. When I mentioned returning to the archives, he asked Bonnie to escort me while he went to speak to the elders. Lord Isak went with him, and I couldn't help but wonder what he'd tell them since I didn't have a complete answer myself.

Once again in the archives, I'd worked with the archivist—a short, stout man with a silver beard that reached his navel—to collect scrolls that alluded to or had runes on them. Bonnie had helped for a short while, climbing ladders to retrieve scrolls. But once the table was full, she'd mumbled an excuse and slipped away while the archivist napped.

I took advantage of the time to ponder what I'd learned. The vision of the monster was unexpected, but it was linked to the runes. Understanding them would give me answers, except the runes were unusual and the scrolls the archivist pulled for me were unhelpful.

I frowned at them, raking my mind to recall what I'd learned in the mage academy. For once, I wished I'd paid more attention to my runic studies. Runes were a symbolic language made of lines and symbols, and because of the intricacies of them, I'd had no interest in it. Memory reminded me that they were marks, usually associated with magic, and often used by corrupt mages. But during the mage wars, the corrupt mages had been brought to justice, and, in the barriers of the unknown world, magic did not exist. Or did it?

With a sigh, I dipped a quill into ink. I wished Lessie were there to discuss. She might have ideas I didn't. But I had to start somewhere, so I wrote a list of what I knew.

Runes appeared at each location, although I'd only seen one. If I looked at the others, I might gain more knowledge. Tomorrow, I needed to get up early and ask Rhyme or Bonnie to escort Lessie and me to each location. Perhaps touching each rune would unleash more visions and provide me with more details, although I didn't want another vision of that monster.

I closed my eyes and an inkling returned, a hint of a nightmare. I'd seen the runes before, and I'd also seen the monster before. *Where had I seen the monster before?*

A wave of fear came over me. One reason the mages spoke out so strongly against using dark magic, like blood magic, was because of what it did to one's self. Mages claimed it opened up a door, gave one's mind over to evil. Was that why I was being haunted by visions of a monster?

Shaking off the speculation, I returned my focus to the runes. One had three wavy lines and resembled an *E* or *W*. The lines were drawn in such a way that it was hard to determine whether the hand had been sloppy or uneven or simply using an ancient tongue. I'd seen something similar the night I ran into the crime lord of the bay, down in the tunnels that crisscrossed the city. Those runes were neatly carved, intended to be read left to right, but it assumed the reader stood in the right direction. What if I had it all wrong?

I turned the scroll to its side and the runes no longer looked like symbols but a picture. The W turned into an M and the picture was clear. It was a mountain. Two peaks and a valley. A breath stole out of my body as clarity pierced my mind. *This* made sense. It depicted a location, likely where the monster had its lair and where the stolen women were hidden. The runes were a clue.

I jerked my head up, excitement tingling through me as I scanned the archives. But I was still alone, the gentle snores of the archivist immune to my discovery.

Biting down my excitement, I turned my attention to the second rune. It initially appeared like three *I*'s, which symbolized the number three. Three was symbolic of completeness. It could indicate the sky, the ground, and everything in-between, or past, present, and future.

When turned, the *I*'s then become three lines stacked on each other. Water? No, the lines were straight and firm, not wavy. What other geography had three firm lines? Puzzling over the runes, I turned the scroll this way and that, hoping to find another meaning. But the mountains stuck with me. If Bonnie or Rhyme returned, I'd confirm with them. This was their land and they might have some ideas about the location of the two mountain peaks and the valley. The runes left after a disappearance could only be the signal that pointed home, and if we could follow it, find it, we would solve the mystery.

Relief poured through me as I sat down.

This wasn't magic. It was detective work, putting two and two together. In less than one afternoon, I'd discovered a key clue and interpreted most of it. Once Rhyme identified the location and sent the warriors to investigate, the women would be found and the mystery solved. Lessie and I could avoid the marriage ceremony and be free to go. Or would we?

We'd seen the secrets of Eyre Heights. We wouldn't be allowed to leave. Marriage to an ice lord was the only way we wouldn't be seen as being useless. This was my new posting, to serve as both a mage and a wife in the ice lands. Resting my chin on my fists, I tried not to think the worst.

The sounds of doors shutting brought me out of my thoughts and I stood, expecting to see either Bonnie or Lessie. Rhyme strode toward me, a look of piqued interest on his face as he surveyed the table laden with scrolls. My thoughts of freedom evaporated as a sensation of wanting breezed through me.

Our initial meeting was an outlier, because I hadn't seen evidence of the stoic, unfriendly warrior since. Instead, I found myself echoing Lessie's words. Lord Rhyme intrigued me and he was easy on the eyes. He was a man of few words yet well spoken, a warrior seeking a challenge yet mysterious. I'd been so wrapped up in my exhaustion and fear, I hadn't considered his perspective. How much choice did *he* have in this arranged marriage? Did he ask for a mage bride?

"Phera, my apologies for leaving you alone for so long. Do you have need of anything?"

The sincerity behind his words disarmed me, and a playful smile hovered on my lips. "Just your opinion."

Rhyme approached the table as I spun the scroll in his direction and pointed to the runes. "Do these look familiar?"

He stared at it a moment, then sat down across from me, tracing the lines of ink. Briefly, I wondered if this was his handwriting. Was he one of the ones who'd rushed to the scene of a disappearance and sketched down the one clue that was left? "Turned like this, it looks like mountain peaks. Why?"

I tapped the scroll. "These aren't runes, it's a picture

of location. I assume where the monster's lair is. If you recognize the landmarks, we'd have a better idea of where the women have disappeared to."

Rhyme stared at the marks, then a low whistle came out of his mouth as he leaped to his feet. "Phera, you're a wonder."

My spirits glowed at the compliment. Still, I watched in puzzlement as he went to one of the shelves. Running his fingers along the scrolls, he pulled one that ran almost the entire length of the table. It was protected in a wood casing, but Rhyme undid the latch and unfurled it on the table. I had to snatch up the scrolls I'd been using to keep them from being covered up.

Rhyme came around to my side, and together, we stared down at a map of what I assumed were the northern lands. There were landmarks and roads, bodies of water, and marks that depicted mountains and forests, animals, and some were people.

"These are the northern lands!" I exclaimed. "I've never seen a map of them."

He stilled beside me. Without looking, I felt his eyes on me. "Do you get any feelings from the map? Does it tell you anything?"

A slight smile played around the edges of my lips and my stomach flip-flopped. I enjoyed being included in the conversation, being the one Rhyme turned to for advice. This kind of communal human interaction was what I'd missed as a prisoner. Tracing my fingertips along the map, I explained. "When a strong emotion is associated with an object or place, I get a sensation. I've never had a vision like the one I had of the monster, though. That was unusual. It makes me wonder if this place is changing my magic."

"Maybe not changing it," Rhyme said. "Maybe emotions are stronger here. What you can do is admirable. I'm aware that my people mistrust mages, and we haven't welcomed them here in years for a reason."

Words danced on my tongue, and instead of swallowing them, I let them out. "Why mage brides? Not simply mages?"

He was quiet for so long, I feared he wouldn't answer my question. But then it came, his voice low as though we might be overhead. "So that you'll be one of us, loyal to your new home, your new family, your new people."

I sucked in a deep breath.

"Marriage is important to us here. We marry for life. We honor, respect, and fight for each other. Living on the edges of the unknown world comes with its benefits and its challenges, but as long as we have each other, we can stand anything. Until now. But you've taken a risk in leaving the southern lands, forsaking your posting and coming here. Once we are bound in marriage, my people will no longer see you as a stranger, but one of us, willing to protect the clan at all costs."

I kept my gaze focused on the map, unwilling to let him see how much those words moved me. "And what about you? What choice did you have?"

His hand rested on my shoulder, turning me toward him. I let the curtain of my hair fall between us, unwilling to let him see my soul. But his fingertips grazed my cheek as he pushed my curls back and tilted my face toward his. "This is my choice. I would do whatever it takes to protect my people. At all costs. It is more than my sworn duty, it is in my blood. It's who I am."

"Then we are the same," I breathed. "Why do you think I became a mage? Magic has a cost, a demand, and one can ignore it and ask for it to be taken away. Or one can step into their calling."

His thumb brushed over my shoulder. "Then I am grateful you answered the call."

A delicious tension hovered between us, as sweet as sugar, and I wanted to lean forward and taste what he might offer.

But a hardness came over his eyes and Rhyme dropped his hand and turned back to the map. When he spoke, his voice was harsh. "Phera, I met with the council and explained what you saw. They agreed to send a group of hunters to search for this monster and its lair."

So soon? I'd barely found a useable clue and they already wanted to rush into the wild. "Will you be joining the hunters?"

"You and me, Lessie and Isak, yes, we'll all go. Now that you've provided a landmark, I'll be able to guide the hunters. It's a three-day journey by yak. I must prepare. And Phera, the council agreed to move up the ceremony. We marry tomorrow."

I felt as though I'd been punched in the stomach. Just when I was warming to him, this blow came. Tomorrow. So soon. There was no time for Lessie and me to plan and prepare. We were out of time.

# Phera

In a daze, I walked the hall back to my chambers. Rhyme had escorted me so far, then gave me directions to take one turn, a flight of stairs, and then I'd find our chambers at the end of the hall. I needed to speak with Lessie, and he told me he'd send Bonnie to bring her to me. All the escorting to and fro was wearing on me, even though I understood how quickly I could become lost in the stone palace. But it also felt like a form of watching me, to ensure I went where I was supposed to.

I hadn't expected news of the wedding to put me in a foul mood. After all, it was expected and it had never been guaranteed that Lessie and I could escape in time. Yet it was the knowledge that by deciphering the runes and finding a clue, I'd sealed my own doom and punishment. Although if I had to marry, Rhyme was a preferred match, and I admitted to myself that I found him attractive, all bearded and stern, with his warrior physique.

I'd misjudged the ice lords. Their focus was on honor, respect, protection, and duty. They were much more reverent of life than any I'd met, and I respected them for that. They weren't after magic or what power could be gained from a mage bride, but clearly wanted Lessie and me to find a new home. To be one of them. I'd misread the situation.

And then something heavy struck my head from behind and I dropped to the ground.

I regained consciousness with a jerk, my skull ringing with pain. I couldn't imagine that I'd been passed out more than a few moments, for faded memories surfaced —falling to the ground, a bag being pulled over my head, my hands bound, then being dragged away and passing out. Now my head lolled forward. In addition to the bag over my head, stifling my breathing, a blindfold was tied tightly around my eyes and a rag stuffed into my mouth. I choked on it, a sudden panic welling up as I struggled to breathe. But flailing was insufficient, for my arms and legs were tied tightly to the back of a chair. Taking a deep breath, I reached for my magic. But there was no water in the air, no moisture to aid my escape.

It was one downfall of mages working alone. Magic was useful, but mages often moved in groups and pairings to offset each other's weaknesses. If Lessie had been with me, she could have picked apart the frayed edges of the rope, allowing them to weaken until escape was possible. But not so with me. If I'd fought, I would be free, but being tied up left me with no options but to hope for mercy.

Suddenly, the bag was snatched off my head and precious air flowed into my nostrils. Before I could enjoy it, a hand yanked my head back and something cold and hard and sharp pressed against my neck. A knife.

"Listen, mage," a harsh female voice whispered. "I'm going to remove the gag. If you scream, I'll cut you. I have questions for you, and you're going to answer them to my satisfaction. And if you don't, I'll cut you."

Here it was. I was abducted and would likely be dead before the night was over. I'd learned in the illegal trade and smuggling businesses how snitches were treated. They were taken, tortured into giving the truth, and then killed. No one trusted a snitch. No one made deals with a snitch. If this strange woman wanted information from me, I needed to get information from her too.

The hand in my hair and the hand holding the blade against my throat did not move, but the gag was taken out of my mouth. So there were two of them, at least, perhaps more. I tried not to panic, but with my vision blinded, my breath came short and fast, fear oozing up my spine. This wasn't the kind of fear I'd felt when taken prisoner—that was a desperate sort of hopelessness and resignation. This fear was tinged with hope and despair.

So I spoke first. "We all want the same thing, to find those missing women. I'm here to help—"

A fist landed in my stomach and I pitched forward, yelping. The hand in my hair yanked me back and pain licked up my skull and abdomen.

"You'll speak when spoken to," the woman hissed. "Open your mouth again except to answer my questions, and it will be worse."

Indeed, the blade dug into my neck, nicking the skin there. I gasped, not proud of the sound that came from my throat. My fingers curled, and I squeezed my eyes shut, searching for moisture in the air. Anything to help me.

"What did you find in the house?"

I licked my dry lips. "It was just a house. I went for

clues. . ." I trailed off as the knife was removed from my neck, then a moment later, it dug into my ribs.

"Mouthy mage. You found something in that house that had you in the archives for hours. Speak."

And then the knife sliced into my skin, a biting sharpness that left me gasping.

"Speak, or the next cut will be deeper."

"Runes. I found runes," I blurted out. One should never give information to a torturer, but I was confused. Didn't they want what I wanted? Or were they the ones who made the women disappear? If so, what were they planning?

The woman dug the knife into the same wound, making me cry out. A cold sweat beaded on my forehead.

"Runes that I believe depict a location, two mountain peaks and a valley, but I haven't interpreted the lines."

"Keep talking or I'll bleed you. What did the monster look like?"

How did this woman know about a monster? Did she hear about it from the council? I explained the monster—its yellow eyes, two horns, stinking breath, hooves for feet, and clawed hands. As I spoke, the vision hovered in front of me, too real, too bitter, while the knife dug into me again. It didn't matter what I said, the woman was going to kill me. Warm blood spilled from my side and bitter tears rolled down my cheeks.

And then the hand on my neck released me and the knife moved away. In one swipe, my hands were free and then my legs. Then the knife was at my back as I was pushed away. Hands outstretched as I put one foot in front of the other. Then silence.

"I know who you are," the voice hissed. "Speak of me and I will silence your lips. Forever. Now go."

The knife withdrew, and with trembling fingers, my hands went to the blindfold. I yanked at it, but it was tied tightly. A sort of frenzy came over me and I ripped at it, limbs trembling, blood dripping down my side.

By the time I got it off, I was alone in a shadowed hall. I spun around, taking in the empty hall behind me and the stone stairs ahead. Pressing a hand to my side, I ran toward them and then up the curving hall, but it was empty too. There was just one door at the end, and I burst through, expecting to find the woman with the knife. But I was back, back in the chambers that Rhyme and I shared, and I was alone.

With shaking fingers, I shut the door and sank onto the carpeted floor, my head spinning. Who was that woman? Why did she hate me? And why did she want the knowledge I held?

# Phera

Inside the bedroom, I discovered a wash basin had been set up by the window, along with a chamber pot. The water was cold, but I welcomed the shock to my senses. My furs were clean, but my dress had a spreading blot of blood on it. The dress was ruined. I took it off, torn between attempting to clean it or hide it, but if Rhyme burst into my bedroom the same way I'd burst into his, a dress soaking in the basin would lead to questions. I needed to hide it. But where?

I mulled over my problem as I cleansed the wound—which wasn't deep—and wrapped a bandage I found in one of the trunks around it. The wound was nasty from the knife pricks, but it had stopped bleeding and the cold water numbed it somewhat. It would likely heal quickly, but leave my side sore for days. I wished I had some of the ointment from the academy. Certain herbs had special properties that soothed the pain of wounds and helped the skin reknit and heal quickly. I'd have to seek a healer, or at least an apothecary. They'd likely be in the city outside of the palace, but I needed someone to escort me, and I wasn't sure who to trust.

Tears welled in my eyes as I finished dressing again and pulled the furs around me. The ruined dress lay balled up on the floor and an idea came to me as I glanced at the balcony. I needed to ensure I was alone.

"Rhyme?" I called out, my voice shakier than I expected. Opening his bedroom door, I glanced around, but it was empty. For now. Returning to the main area, I did the same, but I was alone, which filled me with unease. However, I had water magic at my disposal now. I wouldn't be caught again.

Holding the dress, I slid open the door to the balcony and stepped outside. A chill wind blew my hair back and the air was filled with moisture. Below was a drop, straight down jagged cliffs, to the water crashing upon them. Above and below me was the mountain, without sign of the palace I dwelled in. It had been carved into the very heart of the mountain. What skill.

Lifting the dress, I flung it over the side of the

balcony. The wind caught it, whirling it around, and then came my magic. Using the water in the air, I steered the dress toward the sea until the churning waves caught it and it sank beneath the foamy waters.

Relief settled around my shoulders, followed by sheer exhaustion. I'd just used magic improperly. Not a use that the academy would punish me for, but Mage Margot had often discussed the importance of being productive with magic and not using it for heedless or self-serving purposes. One reason was because magic was for all, and those who were gifted should use it for the benefit of others. The second was because all magic came with a cost, and that cost was exhaustion.

Fatigue crept around me. I needed to sit down and eat while waiting for my strength to return. Yet I lingered on the balcony, watching as something white spun out of the sky. It twirled on the edges of the wind, then hurled in my direction, icy cold kissing my skin.

Snowflakes melted on my bare hands, then brushed my cheekbones. I welcomed the gentle chill, and there in the glow of sunset, the fear around my heart eased. It was easy to understand the desire to live on the edge of the unknown world, where chaos came in its beauty. And this was beautiful.

I stayed outside a while longer, until my fingers were

numb and fatigue drove me in search of food. When I opened the door to the main room, Lessie was sitting in front of the fire and the table was spread with food.

"Lessie!" I cried, relieved to see a friendly face, someone I could trust.

She spun away from the fire. "Phera, I'm glad you're here. Bonnie was adamant, but I wasn't sure. It was so quiet."

"I was changing," I said. "Something happened, Lessie."

"I know. The ceremony will be tomorrow afternoon. Then, the next morning, we'll leave to find the monster's lair. It's all happening so quickly. Too quickly."

"Sit, eat," I told her. "We have to stay strong. There's more."

While we filled our plates, I told her about being kidnapped and questioned. "The worst part is that someone knows who I am, but I don't know who they are. The voice belonged to a woman, but she whispered the entire time, trying to disguise herself, no doubt. And I believe she wasn't working alone."

"This is unacceptable!" Lessie spat, pushing her plate away. "If I'd been there—"

"Lessie, you can't tell Lord Isak nor anyone else about this. We just have to work together to ensure we are escorted to and from wherever we need to go. Besides, we'll leave soon, and then we won't have to watch our backs in the palace."

Lessie shook her head. "I still don't like it. You used to keep a waterskin with you at all times, just in case."

I grimaced. "I used to."

"I will not let this rest. We are going to find the woman who did this to you and ask her the questions. Do you recall anything at all from those moments? I know it's painful, but a smell, a taste in the air, the feel of the stone. Anything?"

I paused. "It wasn't far from the hall that leads to the stairs that lead up here."

"There are five or six halls that split off. I asked Bonnie to show me a bit of the palace, and she did, reluctantly. I imagine there are many places to disappear."

"If we had time to search, perhaps we could find one of the tunnels."

Lessie groaned and wrapped her fingers around a mug. "That's the problem. Time isn't on our side, and I'm curious about this woman and her motives. We're here to help. She doesn't need to know what we know."

"Unless she knows more and she's behind the disappearances," I said.

Lessie stared at the table, considering. "Then why

would she be here? Unless she's helping the women run away and carving the runes into the stone. It is possible that it's all a ruse to trick us."

I picked apart pieces of meat, chewing thoughtfully. "I considered that possibility, too, except that when I touched the runes, I had a vision of a monster. That's unusual. She wouldn't be able to fake that."

"This is a problem. Perhaps it's just an odd coincidence? What if we traced the runes?"

"Lessie, that's dangerous. We don't know what they mean and what our magic might call upon."

"What if the runes summon the monster?"

"I considered whether they're a channel of communication, but I assume it portals the monster back to its lair."

"An assumption, but we can't make assumptions. We need to know for sure."

"What are you suggesting?"

"I don't think the marriages can be avoided, so we go along with them, then we go out into the wild, and once we are there, we draw the runes and wait, see if it summons the monster or something else."

"If it's the monster, we'll be ready with our magic."

"Yes." Lessie grinned.

I reached across the table and squeezed her hand.

This was the Lessie I knew. "I'm glad you're feeling better."

A slow smile spread across her cheeks, and her eyes went bright. "I am. Much better."

I wondered why, but I didn't ask her as I returned to the meal. What we planned to do was dangerous, but it was why I'd become a mage.

# Phera

The air was imbued with a floral scent and the underlying hints of wax melting. I stood at the entrance to the chapel, my curls now tamed, dressed in my wedding day finery. I'd imagined this day long ago, when I was a mere youth, perhaps ten or eleven years of age, before magic awoke within me. Then mage studies overtook my young desires to marry, have a family, and follow in the footsteps of my mother. Magic took me away from family and forced me to rely on the magical community. I'd thought that one day I might fall in love, but I'd ruled out the possibility of marriage.

Lessie had gone before me and I stood alone carrying a bouquet of white flowers—lilies, I thought.

A hand came at my shoulder. "It's time," Bonnie whispered.

I stepped into the entrance and the hundreds of eyes turned to me. These were ice people, strangers, and while they appeared cold and hardened by where they lived, I knew it was an outer shell. There was more, much more to the people than met the eye. They wanted me to be part of their clan, and while I might not know what the future would hold, my actions would shape it.

Last night, while I tossed and turned, nightmares haunting the edges of my sleep, I'd made a vow. I'd come to the north as a punishment, but it was also a fresh start, and I would give myself wholeheartedly to Rhyme and to solving the mystery. Whatever woman was out for me, I'd find the reason and stop her. That's what mages did. My actions alone would seal my place in the mountain of the ice lords.

Music played as I walked down the aisle, alone, a sort of seductive, swaying beat made up of drums and stringed instruments. I trained my gaze on Rhyme and my face warmed. He wore white furs across his shoulders, bands of gold on his arms, and his long hair was braided back. His hand lay on a knife in his belt, while the other rested on the edges of a basin that stood in front of the priest. This was a ceremony of binding and of blood. Magic twitched within me, begging to be released, but I clutched the threads of control, determined not to give in.

Lessie and Isak had already said their vows and stood off to one side, leaving space for Rhyme and I. The walk seemed endless, the watching eyes boring into my back, all the while I knew that one of them was the woman who'd captured me, who'd dug a knife into my side. I held my head high, for I would not be intimidated, especially here, in a land where I'd done nothing wrong.

Rhyme held out his hand to me as I approached and I took it, grateful for his calm presence. There was just something about him—strong, silent, and steady—that eased my nerves. The priest placed his hands over ours and guided them over the basin, and the ceremony began.

It was short yet beautiful. The priest spoke of caring for each other, of love and respect, and it was a message I couldn't recall hearing in the southern lands. Then came the rings. The priest handed me a gold band to put on Rhyme's left hand, but the ring Rhyme slid onto my finger made my eyes go wide. It was a circlet of diamonds around a rounded sapphire, a cluster of gems shining like stars. It was beautiful and had a weight to it, a symbol of the weight of our marriage.

And then came time for the ritual, the binding of our hands, our blood.

Rhyme unsheathed his knife and we pricked our fingers on the blade, then pressed them together, the mingling of our blood symbolizing the two becoming one. I was officially part of the ice lords now, one of them. I didn't expect to feel anything, but as we pressed our hands together and Rhyme's hand rested on my hip, I had a distinct sensation of belonging, of being home. I closed my eyes, letting that sweet feeling linger. At least I had this feeling, this memory to hold on to.

"Let us feast!" the priest roared, and the moment was broken.

The music began again, and we were led out to a hall, where a feast had been prepared. Space was cleared for dancing, and drink flowed freely. I looked for Lessie, but Rhyme kept me by his side, filling my plate with food, keeping my goblet full of wine, and spinning me around the dance floor until I was heady and dizzy and giggling like a fool.

My heart soared, free of all cares, and I realized this was the wedding celebration I never knew that I wanted to have. For as I whirled around the dance floor, shouts of congratulations and welcome came, reaffirming what

I knew—we might be strangers and I might be a mage, but they were willing to open their hearts and welcome me home. Perhaps the ice people were just misunderstood, and they didn't want to be involved with the politics of the southern lands, where greed and corruption spurred the need for mages to be posted in prominent cities.

Eyre Heights was wild and magnificent, sitting on the edges of a dangerous land, but from what I'd seen of it, there was also wealth and comfort, and a strong desire among the people to challenge nature and live among it. This was life, this was freedom, and it was worth fighting for.

It was full dark when Rhyme dragged me away from the merriment, gray eyes darkening as he supported me. "We have an early morning tomorrow. Might as well catch a few hours of sleep."

"Just a few," I giggled, the wine having let down my guard.

"Aye, although I would think about tomorrow when tomorrow comes. Tonight, we keep to tradition and consummate our marriage."

So it would happen. Tonight. My stomach tightened. "Do you always keep to tradition?"

Rhyme pulled me into the circle of his arms, pressing my head against his chest. Dropping his head, he murmured in my ear, "Not always, and especially not with you. But according to legend, a mage's power is strongest after a marriage is consummated, and we are going out into the wild, toward the edges of the unknown lands. My weapons are sharp and my hunters are fast, but you. . ." He trailed off.

"I what?" I asked, intoxicated by his words. His guard had also come down, and he was being honest with me. I didn't want him to stop speaking nor holding me in such a way that made me feel precious.

He stiffened ever so slightly, and even though I couldn't see his face, I felt his hesitation, weighing his words before speaking them. "You must be strong."

Perplexity came over me. *What did he mean?*

"Don't worry about my magic. I am always strong, especially when facing foes."

It wasn't until we reached our chambers that I recalled my bandaged side and worried about how to explain it. But Rhyme did not take me into his bedroom, nor mine. Instead, he lay me down on the couch, settling the cushions around me. The soft firelight lit up his face, making his gold bands shimmer. I held up my hand, watching the light glisten on the jewels. I wasn't vain, but it was the most beautiful piece of jewelry I'd ever owned.

"Rhyme," I whispered.

"Close your eyes. Relax. We'll talk later."

Resting on my elbows, I glanced at my side, but Rhyme was already moving my dress up my legs. His hands on my skin awoke a delightful yet dangerous sensation. When he bent me over the couch, I let him, and closing my eyes, I gave in to the mix of pain and pleasure.

# Phera

The forest sighed as though it were alive and a fog of white hovered over it like the breath of an ice monster. I rode unsteadily on a furry beast—some odd creature called a yak—that looked like a cross between a camel and a cow. It had long, shaggy hair, short horns on top of its head, and trusting eyes that made me want to protect it, even though the creature was three times the size of me. This morning in the barn, Bonnie had told me her name was Rosie. She was steady and faithful and liked carrots as a treat, hence the bundle of carrots wedged in the back of my saddle.

Still, we'd been traveling for hours, and I was sore and exhausted. The events of last night hadn't helped either, and I kept trying to swallow down my disappointment. Rhyme had taken me with a calm control, bringing me to the edge of pleasure. But then he'd kissed me good night and retired. It stung. We were married, yet we had separate rooms and slept in separate beds.

Instead of sleeping, I'd lain awake in bed, then paced the outer room until the fire died into embers. I needed to speak to Rhyme, to explain my expectations, my desires, but I didn't know how to bring it up. Yes, I was supposed to be his mage bride, his wife, one of the ice people, and I had felt that way until he left me alone. His abandonment made me want to cry. I hated how weak and needy I felt.

Up ahead, Rhyme and Isak led the way. We'd left the mountain behind, following a path that zigzagged over open lands. By afternoon, we'd reached the green pines where a mist of white clouds hovered over them. Gray clouds hung heavy, suggesting another impending snowfall. A thin layer already covered the ground, but when the yaks moved over the snow, thin grass displayed again.

Lessie rode ahead of me, followed by Bonnie and two other warriors. The male was called Thane, and the other was female, small and petite, with luscious black hair woven into long braids. She'd lifted her hand to Lessie and me in acknowledgment before mounting up. All the warriors wore pants, jerkins, and furs over them, and carried bows, arrows, knives, swords, or axes.

It felt like too small of a group to hunt a monster, but the main burden of responsibility rested on the shoulders of Lessie and I. She'd winked at me as soon as we spotted each other, and after a quick embrace, we both agreed to speak later. In private. I was burning to know how her wedding night went and whether she felt anything unusual with her magic. For myself, my belly felt swollen and my healing wound itched. Exhaustion, soreness, and disappointment only increased my foul mood.

A lone howl broke the cadence of stillness in the wood, making me shiver at the suggestion of menace.

"The outcropping is just ahead," Rhyme called back, his voice calm and controlled. "We should set up camp. Isak and I will scout ahead and return shortly."

A pang went through me. *Will I have the opportunity to speak privately with Rhyme later?* I assumed we'd share a tent, but now I sucked my cheek, wondering if my assumption was wrong. Customs differed between cities, countries, and stations. Some lords kept their private rooms and a harem of concubines, while others only shared the marriage bed with their brides. Especially after last night, I couldn't make assumptions about Rhyme's expectations. It would only lead to more disappointment.

Rhyme and Isak spurred their snow beasts out of

sight as we arrived at a craggy outpost. Sheltering rocks jutted out of the forest and the trees gave way, providing a shelter from the snow and a lookout, an ideal place to rest while avoiding ambush. The warriors dismounted and started unpacking.

Swinging my leg over the yak, I slid to the ground, wincing as my thighs came back together and my feet hit the snow drifts. Was it possible to be this sore? I wished I had healing magic to ease the pains.

Lessie was by my side in a moment. "We should set up wards," she announced, hooking her arm in mine.

"We're walking the perimeter," I called to Bonnie.

She waved back, but I felt the eyes of the warriors, watching us as we ducked underneath the snowy boughs again. I rubbed my gloved hands together, momentarily wondering if we should have stayed to help set up camp, but the ice warriors had hired us for protection and setting up wards was part of it.

Lessie, who was more skilled with wards, did not start. Instead, she nudged my shoulder. "How was it? Does your magic feel any different?" She certainly hadn't had a disappointing night, for her eyes sparkled and there was a lightness to her, a freedom I hadn't sensed before.

Turning away, I glanced at the wood, which was silent, weighted as though listening for my words. "I'm sore from riding the yak and I feel bloated, like I'm carrying a weight I need to release, but. . .Rhyme is. . ." I trailed off. Kind wasn't the right word, but he wasn't a brute. "He's reserved. I need to get to know him better."

Releasing me, Lessie stepped a few paces away, preparing to set the ward, but instead of working her magic, she asked, "Do you like him?"

A couple of days ago, she'd admitted to admiring Lord Isak, yet I didn't want to utter the words I scarcely dared to think. Speaking them would make them real. "I vowed to give myself wholly to this quest."

"Now you're the one being reserved," Lessie chided.

My hackles went up. "What about you?"

She gave me a shy smile. "Isak was wonderful all night long, and each time was better than the last. It awoke a deeper understanding of magic in me. I can see waves of blue dancing in front of me. I've never felt magic like this before. I believe there was truth associated with the old practices, but I also think there could have been a form of abuse with the arranged marriages. Or perhaps not every mage felt the strengthened magic. I practiced this morning and I think I can send my magic into weapons to make them stronger and faster. Want to see?"

Letting go of me, Lessie closed her eyes and opened her hands. A ripple, like wind, stirred the forest. An aurora of blue light shifted, knocking snow off tree branches and then fading away. "I can see. There's a path where Isak and Rhyme went, and the snow beasts. Back at camp, they are setting up tents and the warriors are taking their watches."

A bitter tang of jealousy sang within, but I pushed it down. Lessie was my best friend. I shouldn't be angry that magic came easily for her, and that Isak had stayed with her all night long to help her cultivate it.

Swallowing down my envy, I asked, "Can you hear what they are saying?"

Lessie opened her eyes. "No, it's just sight, nothing else. Would be awkward to catch someone gossiping about us."

"Nothing new," I shrugged. "Do you see any tracks? Any signs of a monster?"

Lessie frowned. "This is where a sense of smell would be helpful, but I've got nothing."

"We can't have it all," I muttered.

"I'll set up the wards." Lessie stretched out her hands again, her face twisted in concentration.

I remained by her side, studying the wood as she worked. We paused every few paces, covering the distance around the camp, except for the rocks.

Lessie linked her arm back in mine after we finished. "You're awfully quiet. Is something wrong?"

"I've had a headache on and off, and my body is sore."

"Those snow beasts were terribly uncomfortable."

"I agree. I wish I had a pillow to sit on. Their fur isn't as soft as I expected."

"What about your magic? You haven't said much about it."

I grimaced. "It didn't come as easily to me as it did for you."

Lessie nudged me. "That's why we practice. What have you done since last night?"

"Nothing."

"Oh, Phera. Listen, we have some time. Why don't you practice now?"

"I don't want to tire myself further."

"True, but we are about to rest. You can regain your strength at camp. Besides, what if your magic has changed and it doesn't siphon off as much energy anymore?"

She was right. The wood was quiet with plenty of moisture from the thin layer of snowfall, and we hadn't been gone from camp long. With a sigh, I stepped away from her and closed my eyes. I visualized what I wanted and pulled frost out of the air, molding it to my needs. The pressure in my belly eased as I worked, and then came a crack.

Lessie clapped her hands with glee. "Phera!"

I opened my eyes to see a sharp row of icicles sticking out of the ground like teeth. They were as thick as my elbow and the sharp points glistened in the fading light. Bending, I ran my fingers over the sharp edges, relishing the way the points scratched against my gloves.

A wildness overcame me, a dizzying need for more. Involuntarily, I reached for more moisture in the air to carve myself a spear of ice.

"Phera." Lessie's voice caught, and I snapped back to myself. "We should get back."

Magic burned against my will, wild, spiraling, begging to be released. Soreness faded from my body and I felt alive, my skin tingling with energy. Pivoting away from Lessie, I struggled for control, my blood pulsing. Ever so reluctantly, magic bowed to my will and I had a fleeting thought of what would happen if I released it instead of controlling it.

"You're right." Waving my hand, I broke the icicles into shards. "It will be dark soon."

# Phera

We returned to camp before Isak and Rhyme. As we walked up the slope and entered the cove, I felt the gaze of the dark-haired warrior. She sat on a ledge overlooking the encampment, sharpening one of her knives. She nodded when our eyes met in acknowledgment. Nothing more. Recognition came to me slowly. She'd been with the twenty warriors in the outpost when Lessie and I had first arrived. Unlike Bonnie, she wasn't outgoing and friendly, remaining stoic and silent. That's initially what I'd thought of Rhyme, but he'd proven me wrong. Given time, perhaps she would too.

A chill came over me and I moved to the fire. Bonnie fed it with sticks and I stretched out my gloved fingers, letting the heat lick up my arms.

"Do you come out here often?" I asked.

Bonnie shrugged. "We usually come this way to hunt and use this spot as a campsite. For hunting, it's best to come out during the day and get set up to hunt. It gives time for our human smell to fade so that the animals come near. Right before dawn, the beasts feel safe and so they come out. That's when we pounce."

My thoughts went to the monster and the strange runes. According to Bonnie, her sister had been stolen during the evening, when the last light of the day was fading. If the monster were to strike again, it would be now. I let that uncomfortable thought linger, wishing I'd had the opportunity to speak to more witnesses. Rhyme and I had been married so quickly and rushed out to chase after another clue. While I appreciated the hurry, I wished we'd waited to thoroughly understand what we faced instead of rushing out to find the monster's lair.

"Here, have some dried meat while I make a warm drink," Bonnie said, passing me a strip of dried meat.

"Do you need help?" Lessie asked, sitting across from me and accepting some of the dried meat.

I cursed myself for not asking first. Bonnie wasn't our maid. She'd offered to help, likely to stay close to the information about the women who'd vanished, and also because she was curious about mages and magic. That didn't mean I should treat her like a servant.

"No. Why don't you see if Lord Isak and Lord Rhyme have discovered anything useful."

I spun to face the entrance of the camp, my heart skipping as Rhyme and Isak entered, leading their yaks. Isak paused to talk to Thane while Rhyme led the yaks to the side and tied them up next to the others. I joined him, a crashing sensation of hope and heartbreak beating in my breast. The strength of my yearning surprised me.

"What did you see out there?" I asked, rubbing Rosie's soft nose.

"The wood is quiet, no signs of life out there, no tracks. We found nothing unusual, just a carcass the wolves must have feasted on at some point, but vultures had picked the bones dry."

I wished he'd reach out, to touch me, to indicate that he'd been thinking about me as I'd been thinking about him. But he didn't.

Tearing my gaze from him, I caught Lessie and Isak together. He had his arm around her shoulders and brought her in for an embrace, kissing her head. It was quick, but it was enough to show how their friendship was strengthening into something more. So quickly.

The bitter tang of jealousy hit the back of my throat. I struggled to shake it off because Lessie was my best friend and she'd given up so much to leave the comfort of Ethunia with me.

"Who is the dark-haired woman who joined us?" I asked.

"Renava," Rhyme said, feeding his yak a carrot. "She's skilled with the bow, and fast. Her reflexes will serve us well out here."

There were many women who dwelled in the mountain, and many of them hunters and warriors too. My thoughts went to darker places. Had Rhyme planned on marrying one of them before I came along?

"Are we expecting to be attacked?"

He patted the yak on the head, then stepped away. "We are on the edges of the unknown lands. It's best to always be on your guard."

I followed Rhyme back to the fire, his words ringing in my ears, but he didn't ask about my magic or what might have awoken within me. I let the quiet conversation of the others wash over me while I ate in silence, my stomach in knots.

At some point, I recalled that Lessie and I planned to write out the runes to see whether we could summon the monster. However, Lessie did not stray far from Isak's side, and their constant conversation only stoked my jealousy.

It was full dark when I went into the tent, closed the

flap behind me, and hunched over. Still, the low-sloping cloth touched my back. I propped the lantern on a stone and stared at the pallet of furs. It was warmer inside the tent, yet the cold had a way of worming inside me, making my limbs tremble. Rhyme had taken first watch, promising to join me later. Not bothering to undress— what was the point?—I crawled under the covers and closed my eyes, waiting for the soreness to melt away and blissful sleep to claim me.

But it did not come. When I closed my eyes, the darkness hemmed in on all sides and flashes of night-mares made my pulse quicken. The sounds of the night were also unique, the low murmur of voices, the crack-ling of the fire, the wind whistling through the trees. Shivers went up and down my spine, and when the tent flap opened, I almost screamed.

I bolted upright, a ball of white magic hovering on my fingertips as Rhyme raised the lantern, eyes wide. Shamed at my fears, I let the magic melt away, leaving nothing but a hum of tension in the air.

It was Rhyme who broke the awkward silence. "You're still awake."

I leaned back on my elbows. "I couldn't sleep."

"The night does that. It's the darkness, always encroaching to steal one's peace. Especially in the direc-tion we are headed."

Removing his shoes, Rhyme sat down on the edges of the pallet.

I scooted to the side to make room for him. "How far are we from the edges of the unknown lands?"

"Not far, a day or two, and we'll be fully engulfed in the wild."

"You've been there, haven't you? What's it like?"

Rhyme laid down, tucking one hand behind his head, then pivoted on his side to face me. "Wild and unnamable. Uncivilized. There's a feel to it, an edge of chaos. I imagine with your unique abilities, you'll be able to sense it. Where did you live before you became a mage?"

This was the first time he'd asked me about my past. Perhaps it was the dark, breaking down all barriers, or the fear of the unknown we were walking into together. A longing for connection loosened my lips. "I grew up in the farmlands, flat lands with hills and long grasses where one could see for miles and miles. It was barren, empty of people, but plenty of crops and animals to keep us company. Many embraced the opportunity to live in the lowlands, farming peacefully, owning something, working with their hands. That was what my parents wanted, as did my two older brothers. But I wanted more. When I discovered I had magic, I left. I loved my family, but they were settled in their ways and leaving the countryside never appealed to them. It was easy to leave them behind in pursuit of my own goals."

Rhyme made a humming sound and I wasn't sure whether he agreed with my decision. I hadn't asked him about his family and opened my mouth to, but his words interrupted my thoughts.

"And so you left for the Academy of Mages and trained there. Once you graduated, where did you go?"

His question drifted into dangerous territory, but I kept my wits, glossing over details that would give away the precariousness of my situation as I explained. "After graduating from the academy, mages are posted in various cities. Usually in groups of two or three to deal with whatever issues the lord of the land assigns to us. In my case, I was sent to a bayside city." I omitted the name, even though it was unlikely he'd know about the scandal my actions had caused. "Since I'm a water mage, it was an ideal place. It's a beautiful city, half on land and half floating in the waters. One gets around by boat and bridges, and it's a thriving hub for the seafood trade. It had a darker note to it, though. A toxic herb was being smuggled into the city and distributed among the people. It was addictive and created hallucinations, making one feel happy, set apart from the situation, and like they were floating. My task was to find the leader of the smugglers."

"You were successful?" There was a hard edge to his tone.

"Indeed, I was, and then it was time for another position."

"Is that normal, mages moving from city to city, depending on what is needed?"

I hesitated, but this wasn't an interrogation. Rhyme didn't have a reason to guess my dark past. "It depends. Some prefer to stay in one place, while others are nomadic and prefer moving around."

"What do you prefer?"

"I like adventure and a challenge."

"There will be many challenges here."

I watched the light of the lantern flicker over Rhyme's face. Lying side by side and trading words in the dark awoke emotions I thought I'd never feel—the comfort of home, the need to settle down instead of chasing challenges. Yes, there would be many here, but of a different kind than I was used to. The border of the unknown lands made sure of that. Still, it didn't keep me from asking the question. "Why mages? Why now?"

"My people signed a peace treaty, but one day, it won't be enough for the mages of Ethunia. They will come to conquer us, as they did to each city in the southern lands, and we must abide by their rules."

An uncomfortable feeling stirred in my belly. "Is that why the outpost is outside of the city?"

"You're observant. Yes."

"And the mountain serves as a fortress, but it is also a source of wealth. I saw the gold and silver glittering in the natural pools."

Rhyme's voice dropped an octave. "Aye."

"I imagine there are other stones, precious gems, like the one on my ring. Those are plentiful here and rare in the southern lands."

"Was it so easy to see all our secrets?"

"Like you said, I'm observant. I notice the details, what isn't said or pointed out, the placement of objects. It has nothing to do with magic."

"Truthfully, Lord Edwin believes that our time of living in peace on the outskirts will end, so we are being proactive in building up a defense. If mages are here, part of our family, they will fight for us. They will protect us."

"But it is not guaranteed," I pointed out, noting the fallacy in the plan. "Magic does not pass through bloodlines. It is random."

"But magic in the bloodlines makes it more likely, right? Maybe our children will have magic."

A lump swelled in my throat. Children. I hadn't considered that possibility, because while mage brides were rare, mage children were even rarer. Most mages were barren. I guessed it had to do with the energy magic took from us. But such painful words were hard to explain to Rhyme, so I said nothing.

"You're trembling," he said.

"It's cold," I admitted.

His broad hand pressed against my cheek and I drew in a sharp breath, drinking in the sensation of his skin against mine. Closing my eyes, I wished he'd kiss me. I wanted a bit of tenderness from him. Sharing thoughts in that dark warmed my heart, but I craved a physical caress. Did he?

"Come. I will keep you warm this night."

He pulled me into the circle of his arms, my head resting on his chest, listening to the thud of his heartbeat. I anchored myself to him, one arm curved around his chest. We breathed in sync, and before I knew it, I was asleep, and a dreamless night passed.

# Phera

We traveled through the forest, up into the rocky hills, which the yaks navigated without pause, surefooted despite their bulk. I rode with my tongue in my throat, gripping the pommel of the saddle and hoping Rosie wouldn't take any missteps.

She didn't, and two days passed, each one drawing us closer to the summit until we came upon an overpass. A narrow bridge shot out over a gaping hole spanning a ravine. The sound of rushing water came and Rhyme dismounted and walked close to the snow-crusted edge.

"We should lead the yaks across here," he said.

"Are you sure?" came the ghost of Bonnie's whisper. "It's a border bridge. If we cross. . ."

Rhyme pointed ahead. "Look, you can see it from this vantage point."

I dismounted, as did the others, and as we gathered around Rhyme, I saw it. Three lines—a gate, a barrier, a warning. The runes. In the distance, beyond the mist, I made out two mountain peaks in the shape of an *M*. That was where we were going. It was clear we were on the right track, but a sudden twitch of fear went through me. Lessie and I had been distracted with travel and hadn't summoned the monster. But what was the point when we were about to enter its lair?

One of the yaks screamed.

A blur of blackness hurled out of the underbrush and slammed into one of the yaks. It squealed again and started running, taking our supplies with it.

Rhyme had his axe in hand and was running before I took another breath. The warriors moved into a line like dancers, each taking their place. Renava stepped back and nocked an arrow in her bow, while Isak chased after Rhyme. Bonnie drew her sword and stepped forward, searching left and right for more of them. The other warrior, Thane, stood at Bonnie's back, axe in hand.

Lessie and I were embarrassingly slow to dismount and take our stances. As I reached for the moisture in the air, I realized it had been years since we'd fought together, and those times were only during training at the mage academy.

Another black blur moved. It was so fast, it was almost impossible to see, like a ring of smoke dashing by. Was that what they were? Winged creatures?

The yak was still bellowing as the beast took a bite out of it, red blood spraying the thin layer of snow. My stomach roiled as it always did when I sensed pain and discomfort. Steeling myself, I reached for the snow, the water, and then ice. Slowing down everything in my mind, I pivoted slowly while the warriors shouted. Arrows flew, axes swung, and another blur hurled out of the wood. I lifted my hands and impaled it on spikes of ice. The snarl that burst from it was more annoyance than pain, but I'd captured it, and slowly, the darkness took form.

It was a slender beast in the shape of a cat, long claws, a drooling fanged mouth, dark-red eyes that gleamed at me. One of those wilder beasts from tales of the unknown lands. It growled again, dashing claws so deeply into the ground I thought it might dig the icicles free.

Then a blanket of blue surrounded it. Lessie walked forth, chanting, sealing it in a prison of magic. I hesitated, wondering if it were better dead, then turned my attention to the two other felines who were driving back the warriors. They moved quickly, blending in and out of shadow, raking claws across their prey before whirling out of the way of a blade. It wasn't natural, the way they moved, the way they attacked as though they were protecting something.

Were they the guards of the border bridge?

I focused my attention on another one, anticipating where it would move. An arrow twirled into shadow, catching one of its hind legs. It snarled. I lifted the ground, thrusting icicles up to imprison it. A wave of dizziness came over me as Lessie stepped forward again, encasing the second one, and finally, we captured the third.

The warriors stepped back, Bonnie's eyes wide as she faced us.

Renava's mouth was tight as she frowned at the creatures. "We should have killed them. They would have done the same to us."

"It's called mercy," Lessie explained. "Everything dies and so will they, just not today and not by our hands."

"Renava has a point," Thane said. "We have to come back this way. What if they attack again?"

"Then we'll be ready," Rhyme said, his words carrying a final ring to them, ending the discussion.

I watched him move, a limber grace as he pulled the injured yak back, checked its wound, and removed the weight it carried. "She shouldn't travel, not with this wound. The blood will linger in the air and we'll all become prey."

"Send her back," Thane said.

"It's a death sentence for her," Bonnie protested.

"She's strong." Rhyme ran a hand over her horns. "She will protect herself."

Words of protest rose in my own mind. A wounded yak would not make it for three days in the forest. At night, the wolves would circle her, expecting that the blood would have weakened her. They'd wait, they'd prowl, and at the opportune moment, they'd strike. But what could I do? I wasn't a healer.

It was Lessie who stepped forward, eyes bright. "Let me see," she whispered. "My magic protects. Perhaps it can seal the wound so that she might walk without drawing attention to herself."

It was done in a moment, a bubble of blue hovering over the yak's wound. I went up to inspect it, touching the animal's side gently. It did not flinch away or moan in pain.

Leaning close to Lessie, I asked, "How can you sustain this? It's magic. It will draw on your strength."

"I can handle it." She squeezed my hand. "I'd rather not have death on my hands when I could do something to assist."

Her words chilled me as she walked away, joining the others where they prepared to lead the yaks across the bridge, one by one. A strong wind blew, stirring leaf and snow, but my fingers were already numb, spreading throughout my body as I turned over Lessie's words. *I'd rather not have death on my hands when I could do something to assist.*

I had death on my hands. Back in the bay city, I had caused death, fully aware that mages preferred to capture those who committed crimes and bring them to trial. But there hadn't been time. There'd just been me, him, and the cave of runes. He hadn't even confessed, but I had proof because I stood as a witness to his actions, cruel and intentional, actions that had to stop. And so I had pulled the only thing out of the air that I could—blood.

It was a horrible death; he screamed while I drained the blood from his body, and in an act of fury, twisted it into a rope and hung him with it. It was vicious and uncalled for, the act of going to an extreme. I'd let magic rule my temper. Instead of controlling magic, it had controlled me. I'd seen what he'd done, the wreck his hallucination plants had caused people, the ruckus, the madness, and even death. Someone had to pay, and who better than the one responsible?

Discomfort built as Thane led the way across the bridge, Renava following him. I felt Rhyme's eyes on me as Lessie went next, followed by Isak. As he moved, the air shifted and I tasted the ripple of arcane magic. A crack ripped across the bridge and a smattering of stones collapsed into the ravine, sending echoes across it.

"Isak!" Lessie screamed.

The bottom fell out of the bridge.

Isak lurched forward, hands grasping at stones that tumbled out of his hands. The yak he was leading dropped with a scream and bile rose in my throat.

My hands were outstretched before I quite knew what I was doing, gathering snow, ice, whatever I could find, and solidifying it as quickly as I could. Stones grew firm again, not rebuilding themselves but giving him just enough ground to scramble across the last few feet. He collapsed on the other side, staring back at us and the gaping hole that separated Rhyme and me from the others.

Lessie was by his side in a moment, tears streaming down her face. "You're alright," she breathed. "You're fine. I don't know what I would have done if you'd fallen."

Isak pulled her into his arms, embracing her as though she were the one who'd had the close call and almost fallen.

I dropped my hands to my side, a dizzying sense of euphoria coming over me. I was pleased with my actions. Twice in the span of a few moments, I'd proven the value of my magic to the ice warriors.

"Thank you, Lady Phera!" Isak called, his voice echoing across the ravine.

I waved him off. It was nothing.

"How will you get across now?" Lessie shouted.

I considered her question, because there were ways, with magic, but already, a weariness settled in my bones from fighting the shadow cats who still growled behind us, in their traps until. . .until the ice melted, or they broke loose. The decision to let them live suddenly seemed foolish. When given the chance to kill, was it better to kill before being killed, or show mercy? Some viewed mercy as weakness, but it took the strength of restraint and the knowledge that another day to fight would come again, in order to prevent death. Here, I wasn't sure the shadow cats deserved it, but perhaps they were simply protecting their own.

"We'll go uphill a bit to see if there's a narrow

crossing." Rhyme called. "I'll chop down a tree if I have to. Find a safe place to rest. We'll regroup in the morning."

Lessie lifted her hand to wave and I waved back, a growing sense of dread coming over me as they gathered their supplies, the yaks, and ascended over the ridge. Lessie glanced back at me one last time and I gave her a nod.

Rhyme's hand touched my back, drawing me to him. "You did well, Phera."

I leaned into him more than I realized, almost stumbling.

"What is it?" he asked.

Resting a hand on his shoulder, I tilted my face toward his. "Magic. It's a source, a power, but it can't be used without an exchange. I have to pour my energy into magic, and by the end, I grow weary. A few hours and I'll be fine."

His eyes darkened. "Why didn't you tell me?"

I shrugged. "What is there to tell? It is the same for every mage, and the effects don't last long. Obviously, the more magic that is used, the more fatigue there is at the end, but nothing a few hours of rest or a good night's sleep won't fix. At the academy, they pushed us to our limits, to ensure we knew how dire a situation could become if we weren't careful or aware of how much magic we were using. I might be a bit out of practice, but nothing I can't handle."

I realized my mistake the moment the words left my mouth. I was rambling. Why had I said such a thing?

The low tones of his voice sent vibrations through me when he asked that dreaded question. "Why would a mage like you be out of practice?"

*Tell him the truth.* But a half truth hovered on my lips instead. "After my last posting, my skills were not in demand."

I turned away from him to walk up the slope, away from the snarls of the shadow cats, but he caught me around the waist and dragged me firmly against his chest. Cupping my face, he forced me to look up at him and examined me. My heart thudded. I shifted my gaze away, not wanting him to read what lay there.

"You are a wealth of stories and secrets, my mage bride. I find you both frustrating and mesmerizing."

*My mage bride.* Those words were my undoing, and I didn't like the trajectory of the conversation, where it might lead and what I might reveal. Moving my hand up his arm, I pressed my palm against the back of his neck, ever so subtly pushing myself against him, moving our lips closer.

His arm tightened around me, and for a moment, we

were in sync with the wanting, that desire to take a moment to indulge ourselves.

Except that Rhyme had more restraint than I.

He moved his head, angling his lips near my ear instead. "You have your secrets and I have mine. Perhaps for now we keep them and focus on the task at hand."

All my excitement deflated as he released me. The weight of sheer exhaustion sat heavy on my shoulders.

# Phera

We rode Rosie alongside the ravine until it grew dark. I rode behind Rhyme and clung to him, my cheek against the warmth of his shoulder, eyes lulling closed. The ravine boasted a steep drop into what sounded like rushing water below. Short trees and squat bushes grew on either side, but it was clear it was more of a barren area, for even the trees of the forests stood back several feet.

I speculated it was a rift, a barrier between the known and unknown lands. It grew wider at some spots, then narrowed down again. Whoever had built the bridge must have trekked the length of the ravine before picking the ideal place. Shame that such a structure had crumbled so quickly.

"Phera, are you awake?"

Rosie came to a stop. I sat up, peering out at the low-hanging shrubbery.

"I wasn't sleeping," I lied.

Rhyme grunted as he swung down. "I heard you snore once or twice."

My mouth fell open. "I don't snore!" Then I realized this serious ice lord was teasing me. A snort burst from my lips. "I thought you were all serious and solemn, unable to make a joke."

He gave me a rueful smile. "We take our jokes seriously."

Was he opening up to me at last?

Warmth filled me and my skin tingled when he took my hand, helping me off Rosie's back. My sore legs burned and weariness made me hold on to him longer than necessary. All this riding would be my downfall. First the Leviathans, then the yaks. I dearly hoped for a break from riding any beast.

"There's a small outcropping of rock—not much, but it will suffice. I salvaged one of the hammocks. It will be tight sleeping quarters tonight, but better than sleeping on the ground. No fire. We'll do our best to go unnoticed."

"I'm up for an adventure. We'll miss Lessie's wards, but I can sit watch during the night." I dared not voice my fears and ruin the lightness of the moment.

"No need," Rhyme said, swinging his bundle over his shoulder. "Rosie will wake us if she hears anything."

I'd been wrong about how drained I was from using magic. Every step seemed slower than the last as we set up camp, unloaded Rhyme's bag, tied up the hammock, and then, after a meal of dried meat, collapsed inside. Shamelessly, I curled into Rhyme, refusing to reflect on what he did or didn't want. For a moment there, we had been close, and even though he'd dodged my kiss, I still held on to that moment as I fell asleep. I would break down his resistance, little by little, and have the kind of love that Lessie and Isak had apparently found.

The sun was fully up when I awoke, alone in the hammock, gently swaying. Two layers of furs were piled above me and I stretched and sat up, sending the hammock swinging wildly. I slipped out of it, taking in Rosie chewing on dead leaves and tree bark. I gathered everything together as I watched for Rhyme, wondering where he might have gone. We'd had a peaceful night without a worry from the shadow cats, although a few times I had awoken to howls in the distance that never grew nearer.

"I found a crossing," Rhyme called.

I finished folding the blankets and stuffed them into his bundle before facing him. His long hair hung loose, tucked behind his ears, and he carried his axe in hand. My heart squeezed. This man was mine, yet not mine at the same time. But he was handsome, and I was certain he had good intentions. He was kind, not cruel, focused, not lazy, and there was a soft side to him I wanted to see more of.

"Will Rosie be able to cross too?"

"Unfortunately, no. We'll let her nose guide her home."

I nodded, sad to lose the beautiful beast. Going up to Rosie, I rubbed her nose, wishing I had a carrot to give her.

"She'll be fine. It's probably for the best. The unknown lands aren't safe."

Not safe for animals, but nor were they safe for humans. In fact, I wondered if Rosie would fare better in the unknown lands than we would.

"Did you see any of those shadow cats?"

He shook his head. "It's full light, though. I suspect all the nocturnal creatures are hidden in their dens."

"So it's safe, for now," I said.

"In a matter of speaking," he confirmed. Shouldering the bag, he set off alongside the ravine, and, giving Rosie one last pat, I followed. She stared after us with those large doe eyes, chewing as though she didn't have a care in the world. I hoped she wouldn't as she made her way back to Eyre Heights.

Meanwhile, I focused my thoughts on Rhyme and worked up the nerve to ask him questions. If I waited until he started every conversation or opened up to me, I sensed I'd be waiting a long time. I wanted to get to know him better.

"Do you have family in Eyre Heights? I didn't get to meet them."

"Lord Edwin, the clan leader, is my cousin. We grew up together, in a way. I think he always knew he was destined to lead the clan, and he wanted me to work with him. But I was restless, and politics have never appealed to me. I'd rather be out here, hunting, protecting, using my two hands to assist my people in any way that I can."

"No brothers or sisters?"

"Not by blood, but in the clan, everyone grows up together. Isak is as close to me as a brother, even though we aren't related by blood. Bonnie is like a sister to me. The women that disappeared? I know them and their families. My clan is hurting. They are in pain because of these events and. . ." He trailed off, his voice heavy.

The questions about his parents faded on my tongue as I realized I'd opened a wound. What I'd mistaken for resistance to me was merely grief. The clan had experienced significant losses, yet they were closer than I ever imagined.

"Lessie is like a sister to me," I said, offering my side of the story. "I can't imagine what I'd feel like if anything happened to her. She didn't even have to come here, she just volunteered because she knew I was going. That kind of friendship, that kind of bond, can't be shaken."

"A friend indeed." He faced me, just as we entered the ravine where a set of stone steps led down. "What were you running from, that coming here and marrying a stranger was preferable?"

My throat went dry. I stepped back, eyes narrowed. *What did he know?* My vision swam for a moment, and suddenly, I was back there, my hands bound behind me, the magical suppression bracelets against my skin, a bag over my head as they dragged me away, shouting.

"Phera?"

I blinked, the vision fading. My lips trembled. I desperately wanted Rhyme to let me in, to trust me. But it was too much to ask for when I was afraid of letting him know my deepest, darkest secret. Maybe a portion of the truth would help.

"My choices were slim and so I'm making the best of a bad situation. It was come here or never practice magic again, and please don't ask me why. Not yet. The truth is too difficult to speak of. Here, you have everything—a home, a place, people who care about each other—and. . .if I went back south right now, no one who would look for me. No one who would miss me. And I don't say that to garner your pity, so please don't look at me like that. It's like you said earlier, this is the start of the beginning, a chance for mages and ice lords to become one people. I want that."

That distance returned and his expression went carefully blank. After my revelation, I expected a bit more from him, but instead, he backed up a step and gave me a slight bow. "Understood, Lady Phera. We will leave the past where it belongs."

Yet as we continued into the ravine, somehow, I felt like the past was right there with me, sitting on my shoulders, refusing to let me move forward. But if I told Rhyme about corrupting my purpose, what then?

Miserably, I followed him, and it was as though the time we'd spent talking to each other and getting close was erased in the space of a moment.

# Phera

"They have to be around here somewhere. This would be the most logical place to stop, yet they didn't wait for us." Rhyme sighed, pacing in the wooded area, his movement punctured by frustration.

By now, I had a sense of where he preferred to camp, and it was usually where enemies could approach only on one side. But our friends were nowhere. It was noon, and we'd carefully combed the area, returning to where the bridge had fallen and then moving into the wood. Rhyme used a bird call to communicate with Isak, and even though he cupped his hands around his mouth and hooted, no answer came.

The wood was even quieter. As we searched, a sinking sensation built in the pit of my stomach. Something bad had happened. Even with Lessie's protection magic, she hadn't been able to stop what was coming. The collapse of the bridge had been an omen, and we were helpless to stop it.

And then I saw it.

On a rise with no trees, something glowed.

I raced toward it and crashed down on all fours, hoping I wouldn't be sick all over myself. No trees grew on the elevated land, nor did any grass or moss cover it. Instead, it was a slab of rock, and on it were carved the runes. I ran my fingers over them and snatched them back, for they were fresh and still hot to the touch.

"Rhyme!" I called out, a sob building in my throat.

Was it possible that the monster had come for them, that they had *all* been taken? When had it happened? Last night, after Lessie had exhausted her magic?

Hot tears of helplessness blinded my vision, but only for mere seconds. I brushed them away and let fury take over. Taking a deep breath, I held out my palm and laid it flat over the runes. Again came that taste in the air of arcane magic. Pain shot up my arm, but I closed my eyes, letting myself feel. In a flash, I was there.

*The night was dark, but wind fluttered my hair as I rocked back and forth, holding a knife. I kneeled on the slab of rock with fingers outstretched, ready to carve. A need built in my chest as though I would explode, and then came a surge of heat, the scent of animal musk, screams, the crashing of blades and magic. It rolled out of me. Instead of moving, though, I remained still in a crouch, eyes closed, clutching that knife, not daring to move. As though my stealth would bring about my salvation.*

I blinked eyes open and the vision faded.

"Phera?" Rhyme touched my shoulder as I snatched my hand away. When he saw the runes, he dropped to my side. An anguished groan burst from his lips. "No, not this."

"We will find them," I said viciously, my anger rising. "We are close, so close. The monster will not steal our friends from us."

Rhyme took my hand and turned it palm up, examining the runes burned across my palm. They would fade, but they were hard to look at, and they still hurt as though I'd been branded. "What do the runes tell you?"

"I think I saw Lessie, kneeling here when it came for them. I'm not sure what she was doing, but she had her magic ready."

"Did you see the monster?"

"Her eyes were closed. I just felt magic, and there were screams all around her. It was clear they were being attacked."

Rhyme released my hand and stood, drawing his weapon. "We can track them."

I pointed at the runes. "If they went through a portal, it will prove difficult."

"Look."

I stood to get a better view of where Rhyme was pointing. Just beyond the trees were the two mountain peaks with the valley in between. The lair. It was impossible to tell how long it would take, but I hoped that we might arrive before nightfall.

"Let's go," I choked.

The wood remained quiet as we moved through it, a sure and steady pace. I felt nothing but rage—the same rage that had consumed me right before I used blood magic. But today, it was mixed with panic as I thought about Lessie. What if the monster had her and she hadn't rejuvenated enough magic to protect herself?

Mages always worked best in pairs or small groups. It was alone that we often found ourselves in danger. I should have pushed for a way to cross the ravine instead of spending that time with Rhyme. I'd selfishly wanted to get to know him better, and what had it accomplished? It would take more than a night to make him fall in love with me, and I'd already revealed too much of my dark nature.

None of that mattered now. We had to find them

and finish our quest, and only then would Rhyme and I have an honest conversation about our future, if there was even one. . .

A bird call broke us out of our hurried pace.

Rhyme cupped his hands, responding. A light came to his eyes as he turned to me. "It must be Isak. The others are close. Let's hope they are all well."

His call was responded to and then we were running. The wood ended abruptly and burst into a rocky plain where sharp winds blew against the sheer face of the mountain. I gazed up and up and up again, for I'd never seen anything so vast. It was seated in a valley, for the slope led down and then inclined sharply. Stunted undergrowth grew around it and I imagined a hidden path zigzagged back and forth into the beast's lair.

I shivered, not just from the wind but from the up-close view of the mountain. The jagged peaks looked like the horns of a monster, and the wind had a musky scent to it, like blood and body odor.

"Rhyme!" Isak shouted, his voice was high, broken. He waved frantically from the path to the mountain, appearing like nothing more than a shadow. "It took her. Last night. I've been searching all day."

"Did you find access to the lair? Where are the others?"

"Not yet, come help me," Isak said.

Where were the others? Why was Isak alone? Something was wrong, odd, but Rhyme had already started down the slope. Not wanting to be left behind, I followed, despite the warning in my soul. I needed to find Lessie.

I felt the rumble in the mountain right before a boulder tipped over the edge and started to roll toward me. "Wait! Stop!" I shouted. "It's a trap!"

The rock slide continued, stones rolling and clattering like a storm. I spun and reached for the moisture in the air, but it was surprisingly dry. Still, I stretched my magic to its limits as I threw up a barrier to block the rocks. But my magic wasn't meant for protection, it was for attacking, and the rocks rolled on, great stones that would crush me, and Rhyme and Isak.

I ran, still pulling threads of magic. Dimly, I heard someone shouting my name, beckoning me on, but then a rock slammed into my head and I crumbled to the ground.

# Phera

I awoke to a mouth full of blood and a pounding headache. As I leaned over to spit, the darkness of the place settled around me. I lay on a slab of cold rock, underground where daylight did not reach. A torch flickered against an archway, showing me the entrance to the hollow cavern. My heart pounded and my ears rang as I attempted to figure out what had happened.

I'd been hit by the rock slide, but that didn't explain how I'd ended up here. Unless the rocks had carried me into the cave. Except there were none around me. Nothing but the empty chamber.

Was this some nightmare? Some further punishment from the academy? But no, impossible—they'd never come as far as the untamed, unknown lands. I shifted again as my eyes adjusted to the dimness. Behind my panic, I sensed lingering exhaustion and a feeling that someone had taken me, just like the women who had disappeared. I was one of their number now.

I had to find Lessie, and all the other women who'd been taken. They must be somewhere nearby. Closing my eyes, I reached deep within for my well of magic, but the air was so dry. Besides, the very thought made my head hurt more, and so I crouched on the ground, searching for something to use as a weapon.

A thump came, followed by a grunt and heavy breathing. A shadow crept across the wall, revealing horns. The scent of animal musk became strong and the thump turned into the sound of hooves against stone.

I snatched a rock off the ground and tried to make myself small. There was only one way in and out of the cavern. Fool. I should have grabbed the torch. I sprinted for it just as the monster came around the corner, and I was face to face with its chest. Slowly, I lifted my head and intelligent golden eyes, glowering with malice, narrowed at me.

The monster stood at least eight feet tall, maybe more, with horns jutting out of its head, hair covering its face and body. It had the face of a bull, feet of a goat, a whip-like tail, and a thickness to its body, all bulk and muscle. It could snap my neck with just one hand.

I lunged for the torch and swung it around to bash into the monster's chest. A fist cuffed my head and my entire body fell backward. A popping sound rang in my ears as I dropped the torch. The world swirled and my chest went tight, struggling for air. I reached for magic, but nothing came. With a thud of hooves, the monster crossed the floor to me.

A scream came, not from my lips, but from elsewhere. Lessie? And it was just enough. I couldn't faint while Lessie was somewhere else, in pain. Except what was attacking her if the monster was with me?

Gasping for air, I forced myself to move, crawling on all fours as the monster advanced, taking its time to play with me. Its tail swept across my legs, then my back. I didn't know where I was going until I hit the rock I'd been lying on, and when my vision cleared, a crisscross of lines becoming clear. Runes had been carved on the side, and as I swipe my fingers across them, visions flared one after the other in quick succession.

It was too fast for me to comprehend and I didn't wait, because the monster was on my heels and I was under no illusion that I could outrun it. I scrambled onto the rock, hoping to drop down on the other side and hide, but the monster hauled me up with its tail and slammed me down on the rock.

*Not a rock, but a bed. A marriage bed.*

The runes were speaking to me and caught me off guard, then the monster was on top of me, golden eyes leering, slobber dripping from its fangs. I kicked out in rage, my feet hitting its solid bulk. Pain jarred up my leg, forcing me to cry out for relief. While I waited for the spike of agony to die down, the monster tore through my clothing, shredding silk and fur, baring my skin to the cool air.

I flailed in a panic, doing everything I could to escape while the visions from the runes danced behind my eyes. Claws ripped into my skin, fingers traced down my belly, then forced my legs open. That long tongue lolled out, licking up my legs as I thrashed. Pain burned up my legs while blood ran down my sides. A haze of panic made me struggle for escape while deep inside, I knew the monster was going to kill me.

I'd die without saving anyone. I'd failed. Lessie had failed, and the ice warriors had also failed. The monster would continue to ravage the land, clan after clan. Only an army of mages could stop it.

Another scream came, weaker than the first time, and then silence. A terrifying silence.

Emotions tore through me—not hopelessness, but anger, fury at my situation. I needed strength, but the dungeons were dry. There was no water, no snow to fuel my magic. I was on my own. Tears leaked out of my eyes, running down my cheeks, and my thoughts swirled, trying to take me away from what was about to happen.

The monster grunted, preparing to spear me. Why wasn't it tearing me limb from limb?

The dark visions from the runes flashed through my mind again, revealing the truth—I wasn't meant to be a sacrifice, but a bride. A monster's mage bride.

A claw pressed against my chest, holding me down, making it even more difficult to breathe.

"I'm not your mage bride," I wheezed.

The monster stilled.

"I'm already married. There can be no union."

Golden eyes glared at me and there was a darkness to them, a looming evil, as though its mind was not its own.

The pressure on my chest increased, making me gasp. "The magic only works once."

The bullish head of the monster twitched, then it snorted, nostrils flaring as it backed away. Its tail swished. Staggering back two steps, it lifted its head and howled. I felt it deep in my bones, its own rage and frustration, and deceit.

Bile rose in my throat as I gulped in ragged breaths of sour air, aware my ordeal wasn't over yet.

While the monster roared in frustration, I closed my eyes, forcing away the edges of pain and felt for magic. It lay at my core, pulsing to life, the threads reaching for a moisture, a liquid.

Blood. Blood ran off my sides and dripped onto the rock. Blood was life, and the monster was very much alive and full of blood. But blood magic was forbidden. It led to corruption and darkness. Mages weren't trained in using blood magic because it led to instant death. But. . .

If I didn't act quickly, I'd have to endure, and I hadn't come this far to give up and fail. Die I might, but I'd die anyway, with or without blood magic.

The heat of the monster neared, but I kept my eyes closed and let magic take over. It whirled out of me, gathering the droplets of blood from my body and hurling toward the monster. My back arched from the effort as I pulled threads of liquid out of the monster itself, a chant forming in the back of my throat.

The words came to me, from where I did not know, nor did I care. A fiery pain stroked up my body, as though I were being burned alive. But I set my chin, and, keeping my eyes shut, continued to chant until magic exploded out of me and soared, uncontrolled, unstoppable.

A terrible wind swirled and then came a loud cracking sound, like ice melting on a lake. Pieces of rubble fell on top of me, followed by the heavy weight of silence, and nothing more.

I lay still for a long time until my body shook from cold and the aftereffects of magic. I was badly wounded, but still I struggled underneath the rubble, sobbing as I pushed rocks and dirt off me. When I was finally free, I sat up, trembling violently.

The cave was dark as night, with only a luminous glow coming from the walls—a glow that hadn't been there before. It was like moonlight lit my way as I struggled to the floor. It was icy cold, and I groaned, reaching for what remained of my furs, barely enough to cover my nakedness.

I turned toward the entrance and froze.

There, at the foot of the rock, stood the monster, hunched over into a frozen statue. Its eyes were misted over with frost, its tongue lolled out of its mouth, fangs formed into solid icicles, and its claws had frozen in mid-swipe.

I'd turned the monster into ice by freezing its blood.

I heaved, spit and blood dripping from my mouth as

I stumbled to the tunnel. My bare feet scraping the floor made me aware my boots had been stolen. Every move was agony, every breath only heightening it. Hunched over, I held my side and placed one hand on the wall. Taking the right tunnel, I followed it to a series of rough-hewn steps. It was lit with torches, but most of them had gone out, leaving only a few to light my way.

They were too high for me to reach, so I focused on my immediate quest—finding Lessie.

The stairs dead-ended into an open space with a ceiling so low I had to duck to get through. The monster would have had to crawl. But once I stepped through, a cold, pale light met my vision and terror filled me.

I was in a cavern littered with bones. It smelled of burned flesh and blood, and there, on an altar of bodies, lay Lessie. She was at the top, and beneath her were bodies that had been dead for a while, although the cold kept them from rotting quickly. She was half naked, lying with her arms spread out. Burns dotted her arms and her wrists had been slit open, although there was no sign of blood.

I ran to her, tears already blurring my vision as I dragged her off the heap, fumbling for a fur to toss around her shoulder, and feeling for a heartbeat, anything.

"Lessie, Lessie, please don't be dead. Please come back," I begged.

A faint pulse came, but it was barely a relief.

My mind spun. Her screams must have been what I heard when I was with the monster, which meant the monster didn't work alone. Dread coursed through me. Somewhere, there was someone else who was working with the monster, or else. . .

My thoughts whirled, recalling everything that had happened. My blood went cold. The ice warriors whispered tales of the demons of the north who still practiced the old ways, demons who hid in darkness and would not appear unless summoned.

Wrapping Lessie as best I could, I examined the room, my body trembling with weariness. Soon I'd go into shock, but I wasn't sure if I could summon enough strength to find the ice warriors.

On one end was a dark depression, half covered by a rock formation. I limped to it, trying to keep as quiet as possible. My head swam, warning me I'd soon pass out from exhaustion. I needed help—I needed Rhyme.

My throat went tight at the idea of him, at the strength of my longing for him. Everything I thought I was supposed to be was breaking and shattering here in the north. An overwhelm of sensation, of breaking down the structures I'd assembled and relearning everything.

I'd gone too far. I'd used blood magic to free myself and slay a monster—a monster who might have been a facade all along, a puppet used by a puppeteer. An illusion.

Steadying my breath, I peered around the alcove, taking in another doorway. A coldness came, and then pale lights. Daylight came in from above, which meant I must be on a cliff, and whoever had stolen Lessie's blood had already left.

Shuffling a few steps forward, I made it to the doorway that led outside. It was naught but a crack in the stone, enough for me to slip through, but anyone larger could not fit, confirming that it wasn't the monster. A path zigzagged down the cliff, leading into a thick forest.

I waited for my eyes to adjust to the light. Something moved—a shadow of darkness, the pointed cowl of a cloak, a figure shrouded in darkness. At one point, it paused and turned as though to look back. I ducked down, jarring my side, my breath coming in shaking gasps.

We'd been wrong all along. The monster was the least of our worries. Whoever was out there had just escaped and must know we'd stumbled about their secret.

My vision went dizzy and I all but crawled back to

Lessie. I laid down beside her, holding her tight, hoping warmth would keep her alive. Mages were strong, but we could still be killed, if we didn't get help, we'd both die.

My last thought was of Rhyme and what I needed to tell him, but my energy was sapped, my wounds were weeping, and my magical well was empty. I tried to keep my eyes open, but they fluttered shut and I succumbed.

# Rhyme

*The lord of war must bring his bride,*
*A mage with magic to sacrifice alive,*
*To the meeting of sky and land*
*In the shape of a two-fingered hand.*

The words hummed in the back of my mind, words I'd read on a scroll two weeks before the mages arrived. My hand landed on Isak's shoulder as I pulled myself upright. The shelf of rock we'd hidden under was buried under rubble and it shifted as we moved. Would it bring down the entire mountain?

Beside me, Isak let out a groan. "We've doomed them, haven't we? We have to find them."

"We will," I said firmly, and I meant it.

The original plan had been to sacrifice the mages to the monster in the mountain. It wasn't a directive I agreed with nor a plan I wanted to follow, but I was also stuck between doing my duty to my uncle or being kicked out of the clan. Family meant loyalty, honesty, but there was also cruelty associated with it, and it didn't matter if bloodlines were the same. I could still be cast out for disobeying an order.

When the women first started disappearing, Isak and I had gone into the wild, searching for answers. And we'd found them in the form of a horned monster. Rumors had come from other clans, about a developing evil who had decimated their warriors and hunters. It was fast and unstoppable, unable to be vanquished with a force. Something greater was needed. Magic.

The clans of the northern lands had sworn an oath never to bring mages into our midst, for they were evil and brought corruption. It was plain to see that the southern lands were under their sway, and we found it in our best interest to sign the peace treaty they brought to us, to avoid unwanted curiosity. Each time the mages asked for placement at our outpost, the request was denied—until we found the scroll.

Or, to be more exact, the monster handed the scroll directly to me, and when I read it, I didn't know what to think. The monster demanded a mage bride—more specifically, my mage bride. My uncle saw it as a means to an end, a way to use magic to rid ourselves of the problem, and, by default, also rid ourselves of the mages. He sent for two—one to be the sacrifice and the other to be the backup. Since Isak and I had been unharmed by the monster, we were chosen to complete the quest.

I'd tried not to care, to remain stoic and go about my duty, but at some point before the marriage ceremony, my iron will had begun to crumble. The fact of the matter was, Phera was more human than I expected. She wasn't a power-hungry mage, focused only on magic. She was real, thoughtful, and I'd made her my wife, which formed a bond, a covenant between us. Against my better judgment, I'd even taken her to bed, and worse, I wanted to do so again.

I thought I'd hate her and how different she was, having grown up and been corrupted by the southern lands—a place with no respect for nature, focused only on acquiring more wealth, power, magic, lands, and pleasure.

Phera was hiding something, but so was I. Yet I'd seen her dedication, her determination to find the missing women, to ensure we were all safe. Forces still worked against us, but she'd done her best, as had Lessie. I wondered, sometimes, if Isak was under Lessie's power, because he'd completely and utterly fallen for her. Nor did he try to hide it. Thane had spoken with me about it, although no one other than myself, Isak, and Lord Edwin knew about the sacrifice. Lord Edwin was clan leader because his word was law, and he'd persuaded the people that the mages were necessary to enter a new era. Even holding my breath and keeping what I knew to myself, I knew I'd betrayed Phera, perhaps to her death.

We'd entered the realm of the monster, and although I didn't know how it did it, it had probably taken her, distracting us with the rock slide. I gripped my axe. What would it do to her? To Lessie? Were all the women dead?

"I've found a way out," Isak called, yanking me from my stunned reprieve.

"We need to go to the lair and find them," I said, weaving through the wall of rock. It was like a tunnel, wide in some places and narrow in others, the rocks constantly shifting.

"I am with you."

"What about Bonnie, Renava, and Thane? Where did you leave them?"

"When Lessie was taken, I told them to go back. They argued, but eventually saw my reasoning. Bonnie said she'd look for you first and join you."

I frowned. "I didn't pass them. Do you think they got lost?"

"They might have gone south, searching for a way to cross the ravine."

An inkling went through me. I should have seen them, although it was possible that they had slipped by, especially since they were going in the opposite direction. Yet Phera and I had searched all morning without finding any trace of our companions, aside from the runes.

Something was wrong, and my body tensed as the wall of rocks spit us out on the lip of a cave. A sour stench came from it and it stretched on into blackness.

"I think this is it," Isak whispered.

I nodded, understanding the need to keep my voice low too. There was no knowing what might be down there, listening or watching. We were about to enter the belly of the beast.

Isak quickly ripped his shirt and made a makeshift torch while I fumbled with the bundle I'd been carrying for flint. I lit it quickly, then dropped the bundle to the side. There was no need for it in the tunnels, but I took the flint with me. Just in case.

Grasping my axe with both hands, I stepped into the cave with Isak.

We walked toward the back, side by side, before it

narrowed. Isak went first and I followed, disliking the smallness of the area but reminding myself that if this was the lair of the monster, surely it had to fit through the tunnels.

I wasn't sure how long we walked, but my eyes adjusted, growing used to the dimness. Bats flitted by, making small squeaking sounds, but otherwise, it was silent.

Suddenly, Isak dropped the torch and leaped back, bringing up his axe, then growling. "Saints alive," he whispered, then pointed.

Tentatively, I stepped around him, taking in a small room within the tunnels. Isak's torch lay on the ground, burning, and I cursed as I stepped back, alarm racing through me.

"Why isn't it moving?" Isak asked.

Shaking my head, I held up fingers, counting down. As one, we rushed into the room, axes raised. The monster reared before us, its back to us as it lurched over what looked like an altar. Runes were carved around the bottom of it and shreds of clothing lay around it, furs and silks and blood. But the monster itself remained frozen in a crouch, and it didn't move when I slammed my axe into itself. Ice shattered and the wet spray hit my face. I leaped back, wiping my face with my sleeve.

"Something odd is going on here," Isak said out loud, not daring to be quiet anymore.

I stared at the monster, which still hadn't moved. "Bring the torch," I beckoned, going to stand beside the altar as I stared up at our nemesis.

As the light shone across it, understanding came over me. Isak gave a low whistle as the torchlight revealed the monster encased in ice. Its hands were up, claws raised, a snarl across its face as though it had been fighting, moving forward before it was frozen.

"It's. . .dead," Isak said.

Ice. "Phera," I croaked.

Isak whirled around. "She's not here. Nor is Lessie."

The monster was dead. Perhaps the mages had escaped.

"We should search the rest of the cave. . ." I trailed off. Isak understood my meaning. Perhaps we'd find the bones. At least.

The cavern was yawning and wide, with tunnels shooting off in various directions, but it was the torches that lit the way—torches which shouldn't be lit in the cave of a monster. I'd expected to find more bones and blood, shreds of clothing, but aside from the carvings on the walls and the bats we disturbed, the cave was much cleaner than I expected.

Disturbing speculations crawled through my mind,

concerns I'd laid to rest after the horned monster had handed me the scroll demanding a mage bride. Granted, the writing was crude, yet it displayed intelligence. If the monster was able to write, who had taught it? Being dead, the monster could not reveal any more of its secrets, but the cave could.

Once we found the bones, I needed to take down the runes, make a copy of everything, and take it to the archives for transcribing. I needed to know what had happened here and why my clan was targeted. The borders of the unknown lands were ripe with monsters, and bloodshed was a norm my people had come to understand. We knew how to protect ourselves, to hide in the mountain during the winter, to safeguard against the beasts that struck after eve fell. But this was new. Worse, it rang of sorcery.

The tunnel sloped down sharply, forcing us to hold on to the walls and then we were sliding, tumbling down a smooth slope that landed inside a spacious chamber. I blinked against the light. Hundreds of candles were lit, forming a circle around an altar of bodies. In the very middle lay two naked women.

The mages.

A sudden sharpness came to my chest as I raced forward, Isak beside me. A hoarse sound came from his throat as he threw himself down beside them. He picked up Lessie, cradling her body in his arms.

Slumping beside Phera, I found I couldn't breathe. An irate sort of anger was rising, a fury that made my vision swim. She lay on her side, and I gingerly touched her shoulder. She fell on her back without resistance, arms folded around a gash on her waist. Clothes had been stripped from her with what looked like claws, which had raked her sides. Blood was matted on her head and one of her hands was twisted unnaturally.

"Oh, my bride, what has been done to you?"

Her eyelids blinked open, a bolt of fear softening as she recognized me. Her mouth moved, trying to get words out.

"Don't speak. There will be time for words later. I'm going to take you home."

Her head lolled to the side as I covered her with my furs and lifted her up.

# Phera

I faded in and out of consciousness, trying to stay awake so I could tell Rhyme what I'd seen. Someone had bandaged my wounds and laid me on a bed. At least I thought it was a bed, but it was hard, and my body screamed in agony each time I awoke. Also, there was something wrong with my magic, because I couldn't feel it anymore. Each time I woke, a delirium came over me as I tried to distinguish what was real, and what were visions that had been given to me in the monster's lair. There was a smell of iron and blood, and when I cried out, a shadow with long, black hair lifted a cup to my lips, a whisper coaxing me on. "Drink. It will ease the pain."

And so I drank and slept, but the worries continued to circle my mind, escalating into a rigid fear. I was back in the monster's lair and it attacked me again. Its claws split my furs, reopening the wound the woman with the knife had given me. The runes flashed before me.

Mage bride. Sacrifice. Magical blood.

One by one, the clues locked together like a puzzle while I struggled in a sea of my own mind. I needed to tell the truth because the entire clan was in danger. If they'd seen the monster was dead, they would have stopped worrying, stopped protecting themselves, but it was only the first part. There was more to come. I needed to warn the ice warriors.

When I woke next, red hair leaned over me. "Phera!" It was Bonnie. Her face was pale and puffy, as though she'd been crying. "Are you in pain? Here."

She lifted the cup to my lips, but I turned away, despite the dryness that rang in my belly. "Water," I croaked. "Fresh water."

Her forehead wrinkled. "The healer said just to give you medicine."

I was too weak to argue, so I tried to moisten my lips myself. "Rhyme?"

Bonnie hesitated. "He's arguing with the council. I'll find him and bring him to you."

Why the hesitation? My gaze shifted across the room, but I didn't recognize it. Bonnie had mentioned a healer so I must be in the healer's chambers where the sick were laid to be kept close by.

"Lessie?"

Bonnie pressed her lips together and gave a slight shake of her head. "She's not doing well. The medicine doesn't appear to be helping. I'm afraid. . ." She trailed off.

A bright bloom of fear gave me strength. I tapped my fingers against the bed, sending a bolt of pain shooting up my arm. "Water," I repeated. "Water."

My mind was swimming, yet it was so important that Bonnie understood.

Tears of frustration came to my eyes. "Water," I repeated, unable to get more than one word across my lips.

"You're scaring me," Bonnie admitted. "I'll bring water. I promise."

She bolted away, but my energy was sapped and I passed out again.

\* \* \*

The next time I woke, it was to vomit. I leaned over the bed, spilling my guts into a chamber pot that had been placed nearby. I gagged, then stared at my bile, taking in the odd coloring of it. Medicine. *Not medicine.* Poison. I had to find Lessie because it was likely the healer was trying to kill us, slowly poisoning us so that our deaths would look natural.

Everything the Academy of Mages had warned me about the northern lands came flowing back. They were savage lands, and the people themselves lived on the edges of the unknown lands, where monsters and mayhem often ruled. They were used to barbaric ways, but I hadn't sensed that. There was only one person who'd been cruel to me—the person who'd blindfolded me, demanded information, and then knifed me. It was likely the healer was working with them. I couldn't trust anyone, but I needed to save Lessie.

Pulling myself into a sitting position, I moved to swing my legs over the bed and was stopped short. My legs were tied by my ankles to the bed, and on one of my arms was a bracelet—one of the bracelets Mage Idelle had given me. A magic-suppression bracelet, one that I couldn't remove myself.

Anxiety spiked and my gut reaction was to throw myself into trying to free my ankles. Instead, I took a deep breath. I had to think my way out of this. First, I needed water and some sustenance. My body was in pain but I didn't need medicine. It would heal on its own. Secondly, I needed to free myself and find Lessie. When I'd found her in the lair, I knew her life hung in the balance. The fact that she was still alive and fighting was a testimony to her strength, but if I didn't help, she'd lose the battle. Finally, I needed to decide who to trust. Who would believe my tale?

Rhyme had been tightlipped and distant, yet the last night I'd spent with him, there had been a shift, a change. He knew I held a secret, but his was the last face I'd seen in the lair. He'd brought me back when he could have left me there to die. If he were behind this treachery, why bring me here to let me succumb to my wounds?

I wanted to trust him, but my attraction toward him clouded my judgment. Instead of letting feelings guide me, I had to rely on hard facts and truths. Tears of helplessness sprang to my eyes, but I brushed them away, jarring my sprained wrist.

On the table beside me was a jar and an empty cup. Without hesitation, I shoved them off the table. They fell with a crash, shattering into shards of clay. I leaned down as far as my restraints would allow, finger scraping the floor, blood welling up as I snatched up some shards. Tucking them into my fist, I laid back as the curtain moved, and a woman entered the room.

Renava.

I leaned back, trying to appear weak and helpless. Moving my hand, I waved at the jug. "Water," I gasped.

Her expression hardened as her gaze shifted from me to the broken jar. "What a waste." She disappeared for a moment, returning, not with water, but with a broom. She swept up the shards, then glanced back at me. "I'll have to make more."

"Water," I croaked again.

Without a response, she moved away.

I waited, but she did not return, leaving me to wonder at her hostility. If she was the healer, she showed more care toward her potions than her patient.

Gingerly sitting up, I started sawing at the rope. I cut myself many times, and my hands were slick with blood by the time I got the rope to fray. I still had the other side, and my mouth was dry, my tongue stuck to it, but I thought of Lessie and kept working.

Footsteps approached and I laid flat, hiding my bloodied hands under the covers. I closed my eyes, squinting as Rhyme walked into the room. I stayed rigid as I opened my eyes fully, letting him know I was awake.

His expression was troubled as he sat down on the edge of the bed. "Phera, I'm so sorry," he started.

An apology was not what I expected. Was it because he was truly sorry, or because he wanted to throw me off and trick me into trusting him?

"Rhyme." It hurt to say his name. "Water."

"Renava went to make more medicine. She said the jar fell."

I gave my head a sharp shake, which only made my skull pound. "Water," I repeated, more forcefully.

He studied me, then stood and stepped out of the room. Shortly, he returned and poured a cup of water, but instead of giving it to me, he drank, poured again, then held the cup to my lips. Cold, refreshing water flooded my body, awakening my senses. A gnawing hunger plagued me and I drank deeply before he took the cup away.

Pulling myself upright—careful to hide my hands—I leaned my head against the wall, feeling the beginnings of strength return to me. But I was weak and wounded, without magic. If someone wished me harm, they could take me down with no restraint. I had to start somewhere.

I faced Rhyme, looking him in the eye as I formed my question. "Do you trust me?"

Surprise crossed his face. "Don't you want an explanation?"

I shook my head again. There wasn't time. Renava would be back with medicine soon. "Get me out of here. Take me to Lessie."

"The healer said—"

"You are my husband," I interrupted. "It's not over. Someone wants to kill me, then take the clan."

Rhyme's hand went to his belt, where he pulled his knife free. He leaned over me, and for one moment, I thought he might do it, stab the knife into my chest and be done with it. It was a test, and I felt him watching me, knowing what this was. Instead, he removed the blanket, gasping at my bloodied hands and the torn rope. He cut me free, sheathed the knife, and lifted me into his arms. "Tell me what you know."

I could have sobbed, but I wasn't safe yet. "Lessie needs water. It's likely the medicine is poison, meant to slowly kill us."

"Fair. What else?"

I rested my head against his shoulder. He smelled so good and felt strong. *Was I safe with him?* "Food, then we'll talk."

Rhyme turned just as the curtain opened and Renava returned, a jug in hand. Her expression turned carefully blank as she eyed us. "What are you doing?"

To his credit, Rhyme didn't miss a beat. "Phera is better, thanks to your ministrations. I'm taking her back to our chambers."

"She would heal better here, where I can keep an eye on her."

"She's my bride," Rhyme said, then brushed past her.

# Phera

I burned for answers as Rhyme lowered me into the steaming waters. We were down at the natural pool again, and in the past few moments, I'd felt more awake and alert than ever, only adding to my suspicion about being poisoned.

I'd seen it before and recognized the signs. In the city by the bay, I'd come across a woman being fed poison, growing weaker as her body tried to heal. I'd seen the plant used, and heard the refusal to give her fresh water to drink, but never imagined something so terrible would happen to me.

After carrying me out of the sick house, Rhyme took me to Lessie. She appeared so deathly that fear clutched my chest, making it difficult to breathe. Rhyme quickly conferred with Isak, sharing with him the suspicion of poison, and urged him to move her to his chambers. Isak moved instantly. It was clear he was besotted with Lessie, and I felt that twinge of jealously again. I hated myself for being jealous of a friend who was near death, because she was loved. But that was Lessie. She'd done nothing wrong, and if not for me, she wouldn't be in this predicament. I should have fought harder to keep her from following me into doom. There was a reason no one went north, and now I knew why—the unknown lands were treacherous, but so were the ice warriors.

"Better?" Rhyme asked, slipping out of his clothes and joining me. "Since you're a water mage, I thought a bath might help."

Bitterness filled me, but it was hard to hold on to with Rhyme's naked bulk in the water beside me. My gaze strayed over his powerful chest, broad shoulders, and bulging muscles. He was a hardened warrior through and through, and I appreciated his strength.

I held up one arm, showing him the magical suppression bracelet. "Do you know what this is?"

"I haven't seen it before. I assumed one of the healers put it on you to help. They often weave necklaces of herbs or create jewels that hold oils, meant to bring strength and healing to the bearer."

I moved closer to him in the water, holding out my arm for him to see. "I brought a pair of these with me, but I kept them hidden in my bag. They are bracelets used to suppress magic."

"But you're a mage. Why would you bring a means to suppress your magic?"

I held his gaze. "I was supposed to give them to you on our wedding night, so you would have a way to control my magic."

He crossed his arms. "But you kept them hidden."

"I wasn't ready to trust you with that power, but now I have no choice."

"How is that?"

"You're the only one who can take them off and give me my magic back."

"How? I don't have magic."

"There's no need because you're my husband. We are bound by a covenant. A union. All you have to do is speak the word that will unlock them and I will be free to use magic again. The same goes for Lessie. If Isak speaks the words, the magical bracelet suppressing her magic will break free. Are you sure you've never seen this before? Did you put it on me?"

Rhyme moved closer, his expression troubled. "No, I've never seen it before. Now tell me the words to speak and I will set you free."

He was so quick to believe me, to support me, but there was more I wanted him to hear. I glanced around the pool, but we were seemingly alone. "Rhyme, if it wasn't you, it had to be someone else with magic. Someone who had access to my bag, who knew where I'd be and could slip in and stop me. Who here has magic?"

"No one." He shook his head fiercely. "There is no magic here. You must be mistaken."

Instead of responding, I sank deeper into the water, letting it hover around my chin. The warmth felt good, soothing the anger of my wounds. Magic flowing through my body would feel even better. "The word *lantana* will set me free."

"*Lantana*," he repeated.

The bracelet broke open with a sigh, and I caught it before it fell into the water. The slow pulse of magic returned, but it was just as weak as I.

I cupped it in my fingers as Rhyme's hand grazed my hips, pulling me toward him. A slow pinch of desire started to build, and I leaned toward him, allowing myself to feel, to want.

He pressed his head against mine, ever so gently, whispering, "I'm sorry it came to this, Phera. I should have been honest with you from the start, and I should let you go free. Fly back to the southern lands where there is safety. Forget about this, forget about us."

My heart pounded because none of his words were possible. "But I can't forget about you."

"I've brought you nothing but sorrow."

"It's not your fault. I came here to do what any mage would do—find the truth, and I'm close. *We* are close."

"Phera, I swear to you I will do my best, but I'm not sure if I can save you."

I pulled away. "What do you speak of?"

He released me, but it was reluctant. "Let us retire to our chambers and I will tell you the truth."

# Phera

Back in our rooms, I settled into the cushions of the sofa, letting the heat of the fire warm me. Rhyme wrapped a loose blanket around my body and I watched him silently, appreciating his care and concern for me. Perhaps his slow and steady way was better than the passion that burned between Isak and Lessie. I resolved to put away my emotions and listen with an open mind. Love had nothing to do with what was happening now.

Rhyme eased himself down on the other side of the sofa, facing me. His wet hair lay across his shoulders, drying, and he'd put on a simple linen shirt which hung loose over his trousers. For once, he didn't appear like a warrior, for his weapons lay on the table. He was just a man, yet looking at him made my heart ache. For so long, I'd wanted a place to belong, and this might have been my chance, except he was willing to end the marriage and send me away. For my own safety.

Rhyme stroked his jaw, smoothening down the edges of his beard. "I've seen the monster before."

I stiffened, but continued to pick at the bread and cheese and dried meat on the tray before me. I'd need my strength and so I needed to eat. The hot bath and release of my magic had helped, but my body was still healing and the poisonous drink had sapped my energy.

"When the women started disappearing, Lord Edwin appointed me to investigate. I assumed it was a beast dragging the women away, even though there was no sign of them. Isak thought that perhaps the women had run, or were hiding. Regardless, we went into the wild and we found nothing but death. You should know that there are many clans in the northern lands. Most of them are family and bloodline-based groups of only a hundred. The larger ones, like this one, have no more than two or three hundred. We've made alliances to come to each other's aid if need be. But Isak and I went as far as the western hills. Homes had been abandoned, animals slain. A menace was out there, attacking. Word came from a faraway clan that they were taking refuge in the mountains because of a monster that attacked without regard for life. The lowlands were empty, and they were preparing for war. We did the same."

My stomach roiled. I put down the hunk of bread, dread filling me. "How long ago was this?"

"Two months ago. Isak and I were gone a month hunting. We found no answers, but on our way back, the monster attacked us."

*He is still alive, though. Why?*

"It had a message for us, written on a scroll. A demand for a mage bride as a sacrifice."

It was too hard to look at him. Jaw set, I stared at the fire, willing my anger to settle into something reasonable. Lessie and I had been set up. Did the Academy of Mages know? Had the ice lords asked for mages they could easily send to their deaths? Mages who wouldn't be missed? And Rhyme, what about his role in the despicable act? No wonder he'd been stoic and reserved. Was the reason he slept with me during our wedding night because he was too drunk on spirits to restrain himself?

"Isak and I took the message back to Lord Edwin, seeking advice. More women had disappeared while we were gone and the clan was panicked, seeking an answer. Lord Edwin decided we'd appease the people, tell them we were asking mages to help us. As expected, the elders met the request with resistance. We'd vowed never to bring the wildness and corruption of magic here. Lord Edwin talked them down, explaining the extreme circumstances, how never in our historic past has there been a need this great. He even told them we'd accept not one but two mage brides to intermix with our people and bring magic to our lands—magic that would be controlled."

"You said those words to me—mages that would be part of your clan," I spat, unable to keep the fury out of my tone. "You said you wanted a bride to learn your ways and children who might have magic. All those things you told me were lies."

"Phera, I make no excuses for the role I played in betraying you. I am sorry. I should have stood up to Lord Edwin sooner, instead of being deceptive. I wanted the life of a hunter instead of a warrior. I wanted to be free of this mountain and the politics that come with working for Lord Edwin. He promised that if I followed his orders this one last time, I'd be free of the debt I owed him. And so I agreed, despite the warnings in my heart. I hoped that you and Lady Lessie could defeat the monster with magic. From there, Isak and I were going to sneak you back to the outpost and send you south, claiming that you died while slaying the monster. Except that's not what happened."

I glared at him, impulse making me want to hurl the plate of food at his face while logic made me question if his words were true. "When were you going to tell me about this plan?"

"You were never supposed to know about the monster, the letter. . . Assuming you'd done your duty, you could return to the Academy of Mages and take another post. It's not too late, Phera. As soon as you are able to fly, I will sneak you out of here. You can escape this plight."

*He wants to get rid of me.* I gave a bitter laugh, unable to keep the sarcasm out of my words. "How chivalrous of you to offer a way out, but it's far too late for that."

"I can claim that you succumbed to your wounds. It's not a far-off claim, and I have enough to pay off the flight master."

I judged him that I sat there, hating what he'd done, but I'd been duplicitous as well. I had nothing to lose, no need to salvage a marriage that was already broken by secrets. Still, it was too hard to look at him, so I kept my face toward the fire. "When I was in the monster's lair, it tried to take me as its mage bride. While I was fighting it, I heard screaming. Lessie was trying to fight someone off, but I was with the monster. Out of desperation, I used dark magic, blood magic, to freeze its blood."

"I saw what you did. The monster is dead."

I shook my head. "The monster is dead, but it was never about the monster. When I found Lessie, she'd been. . .drained of blood, her body used as a runic sacrifice. That room she was held in had another entrance, and when I went to it, I saw a hooded figure hurrying down the slope. Rhyme, someone else is behind all of this, and they have magic. Whatever they wanted, they got, and they will strike again soon. From what I've seen of your clan, they are skilled and wealthy. What would be gained with a shift in power?"

"There is nothing to be gained."

"There's *always* something to be gained," I argued. "You said it yourself. Lord Edwin offered you what you want, and even if you have to fake my death, you agreed to it. Don't you see? Everyone has something they will bargain for, and magic has been among you this entire time. If Lessie and I leave now, it is likely we will leave you to your death. Besides, I *can't* leave."

Rhyme was silent for so long, I drew my gaze from the fire and faced him. He sat upright, leaning forward, stroking his beard as though it would give him answers. The pained look on his face made my hard heart soften, but I forced that weakness away. Yet it lingered, the awareness that despite it all, despite everything, I wanted to help him.

"If it is the marriage that concerns you, I will not hold you to it."

I stood, unable to sit with him anymore. The blanket slipped off one shoulder, baring it to him, and I grabbed it, wrenching my sprained wrist. Tears of self-pity came to my eyes. "You've made it quite clear that you want to get rid of me and this sham of a marriage. If you don't want my help, fine. I will leave, but I can't go south. They'll lock me up. Did you ever wonder why I brought bracelets that suppress my magic? It's because I'm a corrupt mage. I was given a choice—a life in the dungeons or coming here. They didn't tell me I was to be a mage bride, not until it was too late. Worst of all, Lessie did nothing wrong. She chose to be here because *I'm* here. This is supposed to be my punishment, and a punishment it is. A husband who betrays me, who can barely look at me, who can't wait to fake my death. A people who have plans to kill me. My best friend is dying, and I'm homeless and alone, surrounded by treachery."

I pressed my hands over my mouth and spun away from him, hating myself for my outburst and how self-centered it sounded. But it was more than just him—it was everything that had happened to me the past three months, proving to me over and over again that I was not worthy, I was not enough, and nothing I said or did would be enough to bring redemption. Worst, I hadn't limited my use of blood magic to what had happened on the bay—I'd used it again on the monster. Without remorse. I wasn't sorry for what I'd done to protect others, and that second act, if discovered by the academy, would seal my death sentence. If I went back and they found out what I did, I'd be made an example of, my death the event of the season to remind mages of what would happen if they broke the treaty and used dark magic.

Rhyme's hand grazed my bare shoulder then dropped to my waist, spinning me to face him. He sat on the back of the sofa and brought me between his knees. Sitting down, he was right at eye level, and when he cupped my cheek, raising my face to his, the blanket fell from my shoulders, exposing my breasts. But he didn't look down, nor did his face heat with lust. There was a depth to his gaze, a stillness in his movements.

"You mistake me, Phera. You've taken my words, my silence, my reserve toward you as indifference. From the moment we met, I've been curious about you, humbled that I would have a mage bride. I've heard nothing but stories of the power of mages, the feats they accomplished. I did not oppose bringing mages here. It was an old treaty, an old idea, but I was afraid of how my people would treat you, the prejudice and fears that have been passed down from generation to generation. Most knowledge about mages is based on a terrible treachery that happened in the past. But I've seen you in action, and you've told me your darkest secret, and I've told you mine. If I have been reserved with you, it's because I didn't want to get to know the woman I'd have to send away."

"Do you mean that?" I asked, searching the depths of his gaze for a lie. "It was your intent all along to use me to slay the monster, then fake my death and send me back."

"I swear it to be true."

My chest rose and fell as I let the words sink in. "Then we have a problem," I said. "Someone still wants to kill me, and by angering the healers, you might have put yourself in their crosshairs. So to speak."

His eyebrows lifted in amusement. "Crosshairs? I've never heard that phrase. But speaking of bow and arrows, it makes a deal of sense. What do you suggest?"

A wave of weariness came over me. "I need to sleep and figure out what to do next. Are we safe here?"

"For now, but I can make arrangements."

"Do what you must. My strength is failing, but wake me in the morning, Rhyme. Time is short."

He lifted me up and carried me, not to my bed but to his, where he laid me down. His fingers tiptoed across my chest as he pulled the blankets over me. I reached for him, feeling comforted, as if I had a place to belong.

He took my hand in his, squeezing it gently. "Phera, you should know, I want you to stay."

# Rhyme

After what Phera had revealed to me, walking the curving stone halls of Eyre Heights made me feel like a thief. My hand kept going to my belt where my curved knife was hidden, just in case someone tried to sneak up on me. It was hard not to think about assassins. Would my uncle stoop that low?

I believed the best of him, even though he was strict and demanding, as any other clan lord in his place would have been. Yet I knew assumptions could be blinding, so I let the truth of Phera's tale worm its way around my chest.

Erring on caution, I'd had Isak move into my chambers with Lessie. I couldn't chance leaving the mages alone. What if someone took a knife and finished what the monster had started? It was fortuitous that Isak hadn't left Lessie's side since he found her in the cave. Not once. I'd even brought him food. That act of loyalty had likely saved her.

I'd judged him for wanting a wife, for enjoying his mage bride when we had work to do. I'd been wrong, for Phera had misjudged my silence, my distance, as dislike. But I did not want to get to know a bride I was meant to send away. I wanted to give her a chance to live, and her acknowledgment of being a criminal—according to the Academy of Mages—was not enough to change my view of her. However, it made some things clear—she was willing to go to extremes for the truth.

Rubbing my neck, I pushed open the doors to the great hall where the elders gathered during the day. The room had a bowl-like shape and since there were no windows, razor-sharp white light shone in from the glass rooftop. Artisans had worked hard to make it a place full of light, yet the glass was thick enough to shield against the cold, and the layers of snow and ice that built on it during the fall and winter. On a clear day, a view of the mountain ranges could be seen, but today, gray clouds covered the sky, warning of more snow.

The low murmur of voices filled the room with a musical cadence. Lords sat or stood around various tables scattered across the room, some discussing intently, while others appeared more relaxed, focused on a game of cards or dice. An enormous fireplace warmed it, and the scent of something smoky and sweet drifted to my nose. Saliva filled my mouth.

It would be easy to pretend the mages had died. I could become one of the lords there for a drink, a meal, or a mindless game. But I'd never been one of them and I'd come with a reason. Ignoring the eyes that lingered on me, I strode to Lord Edwin's table and took a seat.

He scowled at me. "Bold of you to assume you were invited to my table, Lord Rhyme."

Such scorn in his words. "Since the invite was not forthcoming, I've invited myself."

Lord Edwin turned to the men on either side of him. "Dismissed. Let me have a private word with my nephew."

Throwing in our family tie wasn't an endearment. I felt my hackles rise and fought to keep my temper. Lord Edwin was fond of goading me.

Once the other men were gone, I looked him square in the eye. "I came to speak with you about my mage bride. The monster is dead. The mages live. What do you make of that?"

He didn't flinch. "You have a wife now. Go settle in the lowlands by the sea, as you wish. You have fulfilled your duty as a warrior."

Angela J. Ford

"Am I released because I have fulfilled my duty, or because you want the mages to leave the safety of Eyre Heights and retire, where some unfortunate accident might happen in the lowlands?"

"I said what I said without making assumptions. It is you who assumed I meant my words in ill favor. Must you always do that? I said what I said, and I meant it. Go or stay here. It means nothing to me."

*I* meant nothing to him. I was simply a means to an end, and I'd do what he asked, because I owed him. My parents had been slain in a raid, and Lord Edwin had taken me in when I was twelve years old. My parents had raised me, but he ensured I had a home until I became a man, fully ready to take care of myself. The years I'd taken from him, I gave back as a warrior. He was just that—my uncle, not a father or a friend, merely a member of my bloodline.

"The monster might be dead, but this isn't over."

Now I had his attention. "What do you mean? I sent the warriors out. They found the monster's lair and brought back its horns as trophy. We buried our dead, the people are grieving. There is nothing left."

"The mage believes that someone using magic is behind the disappearances and the monster was only a distraction, a means to an end during the first phase. Whoever this individual is, or perhaps a group of indi-

222

viduals, they got what they wanted. Now they need the mages to die so they can move forward without resistance."

"What proof is there?"

"Phera saw a hooded figure fleeing from the monster's lair." I failed to mention the magical bracelets that suppressed magic. I suspected the story about her criminal activity wasn't something she wanted spread throughout Eyre Heights. She'd come here for a fresh start, to escape those who judged her, and it was bold of her to entrust me with her secret. The acknowledgment of her shortcomings only made me trust her more. She actually wanted to help stop whatever was happening. She truly was selfless, a protector of the people despite the harm it placed her in.

Lord Edwin leaned back and crossed his arms, his words full of scorn. "She happened to see someone fleeing? That means nothing. It could have been someone else who escaped from the monster."

I hadn't considered that. I needed to question Phera more closely. Could it have been her imagination? She'd had a head injury and lost a lot of blood. But then there was the fact that she'd heard screams while she was fighting the monster. Screams from someone who was being attacked?

"Fair enough. But you have to admit it makes sense.

The odd runes, the strange vanishings, the scroll the monster gave us with its demands. Monsters don't read or write."

"Don't be a fool. You know where we dwell, on the edges of the unknown lands where supernatural beings always seek to pull us into their sway. Be strong and stand up for yourself. So the monster was intelligent. It is strange but not unusual."

"Uncle, I know where we live, but I think there is some validity to this. I'd like to continue searching. If there is a threat to our clan, I would see it put to an end. The mages can help."

His nostrils flared. "The mages are supposed to be dead."

"Would you have me slay my bride?"

"No, we are not murderers. Keep searching, then. Just know the elders will not stand for this. They may have agreed to bring mages into our midst for this dire circumstance. . ." He trailed off, realizing he'd said too much.

The unsaid words hung between us, so slowly I filled them in. "It would be helpful if the people believe the mages are dead."

"Why?"

"Whoever is behind this will be less cautious if they

don't have to worry about someone with magic coming after them."

Lord Edwin sat back. For a moment, a tiredness came over his face. "We never should have brought them here. We've always dealt with our problems ourselves, and I let myself be persuaded. Never again."

I sat with those words, turning them over. He *let* himself be persuaded? All along, I'd assumed he was the one who demanded we bring the mages in, who swayed the council of elders, and blackmailed Isak and me into taking them as brides. We'd stood up in front of the entire clan and married them, took them as our own. I'd fully believed it was his decision.

"Who persuaded you, Uncle?"

His face turned red. "Does it matter?"

It did, but I didn't press the matter. "Uncle, if someone with magic were to be in our midst, how would they hide?"

"Impossible. No one with magic in the blood is left. They were all slaughtered long ago."

*But what if. . .*

We all knew the tale because it was part of our history. Decades ago, magic was in the northern world. Mages were born and magic was wild and rampant because there was no such thing as the Academy of

Mages, nothing to keep the balance of powers in check. Mages rose to power and ruled the north with a ruthless hand. Thus, in secret, the clans of ice lords were born, first as skilled hunters who chased down mages and killed them. As the story went, bloodlust drove them and they hunted down the mages, cutting them off from each other, and slaying them one by one, searching for every one of their bloodline. It was a massacre, the part of our history no one was proud of. There were only rumors of the lengths the ice lords went through to ensure magic did not touch this land again, and the oath that was sworn.

It was a bloody tale, full of revenge and evil, one I hoped the mages of the southern lands would never hear. If they'd known what was done in the past, they never would have set an outpost.

"I would urge vigilance at this time, just until we know that this is over. For good."

Lord Edwin waved his hands. "You've soured my attitude enough for today. Go and do what you think is best, but report to me in the privacy of my chambers. No one needs to know what is going on. And if you must, take the mages away."

I stood with a sudden urge to give him a mock bow. Lord Edwin gave orders as though he were king, yet no one challenged him because he stood a head and shoulders above everyone. Even the clans did not oppose us.

Although the land was still ripe with mystery, with wild animals and nature seeking to take back the land, we had the mountain, a source of wealth and riches. It inspired trade and kept the other clans on our side.

I took my leave from Lord Edwin, thinking through a plan of action. If, indeed, someone from the line of mages had survived, why wait until now to strike? To act? It had been at least two hundred years since then, not long enough for any to survive.

And then I recalled the seer.

# Phera

It took three days to purge the poison from my body. Three days of sweats, of tossing, turning, hot then cold, unable to keep anything down for more than a few hours. Finally, on the fourth day, I woke with a hunger for food, a clarity to my mind. My body was still sore, weak and healing from the wounds, but strength came from within. I rose and went to Lessie's side, for she and Isak had taken my room. When Isak had first moved her in, she appeared near death. Now she sat up in bed, her hair down around her shoulders, the scent of lilac drifting from her. She wore a clean nightgown, and it was clear she'd had a bath.

She smiled at me, and even though weariness settled like a halo around her, a spark of life lit her eyes. "Phera." Her voice was scratchy from disuse.

"Where are the men?" I asked.

She jerked her chin toward the door. "Discussing. I suspect they do daily. I understand you're responsible for saving my life. Thank you, Phera."

"Lord Isak and Lord Rhyme played a part in our survival too," I explained.

Lessie picked at the furs of the blanket. "Did you tell them what happened in the monster's lair?"

I sat down on the edge of the bed, my throat thick. "Some, but I haven't heard your side of the story. What happened after the bridge collapsed?"

"We went on, searching for a place to make camp. Lord Thane found a place at the back of a hill and an argument broke out. Isak and I wanted to find higher land, especially being across the border and in the unknown lands." She shrugged. "You know the rumors."

"We saw for ourselves when the shadow cats attacked. "

"We did. I'd forgotten about it."

"Did you move to higher land?"

"No. Darkness fell early. It surprised us. I wanted to set up wards, but my magic was exhausted from earlier. I told Isak I needed to rest, and to wake me in a few hours and I'd set them up."

"So you went to sleep?"

Lessie grimaced. "I did, and when I woke, the camp

was under attack. I ran out, and all I recall was fire, shapes moving in the trees, and then that terrible, horned monster. It snatched me. Its breath was so foul and. . ." Gagging, she trailed off.

My pulse pounded at the reminder. "Rhyme and I found the place where you were attacked, but no signs of the camp. Everything was gone, including the yaks, as though it had never been. But I found the stone with the runes on it."

"What stone? We were in the forest."

I closed my eyes. "No, I remember because I had a vision when I touched the runes. It was a forest, but the hilltop was stone, and on top of it were the runes. In the vision, I was. . .you. I was kneeling on the stone, holding a knife and the sounds of battle were around me. It had to be a recent incident. It flashed as soon as I touched the runes."

"There was someone on the hilltop when the monster snatched me. I remember that, but. . .it wasn't me. I recall struggling, and the monster was carrying me uphill. Phera, it must have been going to the stone, so it could use the runes to reach its lair again. Or perhaps it didn't need to because the lair was so close. Whoever's vision you saw. . ."

We looked at each other, both thinking the same thing, but hesitant to say the words out loud.

231

Lessie's brows knitted together. "What I don't understand, though, is how the monster got to you."

I quickly filled her in about the search Rhyme and I had conducted, the rock slide, and ended with fighting the monster and finding her.

"I thought you were dead," I admitted. "But there was someone else there, a hooded figure who fled when I approached."

Lessie shuddered. "I thought I was going to be eaten by the monster, but when I woke up, I was tied to an altar and someone was bleeding me. I couldn't figure out who it was. They remained hooded. I believe their face was masked and then my vision started going."

"Is there anything at all you recall about them? A scent? A sound? Anything that would help us find them?"

"It smelled so much like blood—blood and iron. I was determined to escape, but the blood loss made me weak. The person kept chanting, though."

"Like a magical ritual."

"Exactly. I wish I had more to say, to identify this person, but I can't recall."

"You were free when I found you. Maybe you fought back," I suggested.

Lessie tapped her fingers on the blankets, an awareness spreading across her face. "I don't recall seeing the women."

"Lessie, there were bodies, an altar of them," I said gently. "It was terrible."

Lessie grimaced. "I thought that was some dream, but there was something else." She snapped her fingers, trying to remember. "I don't recall any animal bones, and it smelled like blood, not like the cave of a wild animal, with death and decay."

I nodded slowly. "What are you thinking?"

"Whoever is responsible was using the monster as a decoy."

"I thought as much too."

"It's someone here, because they captured you and held you, demanding to know what you knew. That way they could use the information to stay hidden. To deceive us."

"What if it's someone here who discovered they have magic? Or one of the dark mages from the years of corruption escaped and came here?" I mused.

"We just have to find them before they find us."

I glanced at her arm, where the magical suppression bracelet had been removed. "They already found us," I reminded her. "I think it's one of the healers. Who else put the magical suppression bracelets on us? Who would know what they are aside from a mage who'd seen them before?"

"Did Mage Idelle tell anyone?"

"She conferred with Lord Edwin and we never saw her leave. But. . .from what I know of her from the academy, I don't believe that was her intent. Besides, what was happening here started long before we arrived."

I closed my eyes. Thinking through. "It's a woman."

"Bonnie? Renava?"

Sadness filled me. "Ever since we've been here, Bonnie has stayed close to us. She volunteered."

"I recall her visiting me when I was in and out of consciousness."

"There's something about Renava." I let the thought hang.

"We need to find her and question her."

# Phera

"We need to talk," Rhyme said, sitting at the head of the bed and leaning back against the wall.

I wrapped a shawl around my shoulders and sat down across from him, curling my feet under me. "About what's going on?" I asked carefully.

I hadn't shared the takeaways from my conversation with Lessie with him yet. I had questions about Renava and wondered if he would be able to answer them or if it would be better to take a risk and question Bonnie. Problem was, I wasn't sure where Bonnie's loyalties lay.

"About us."

My heart sank.

Rhyme and I still had a tentative relationship. He'd taken care of me while I was recovering and while I knew he wanted me to stay, we hadn't discussed what a future together might look like. It was easier to speak of monsters and clues, suspicions and danger, than to discuss matters of the heart.

I eyed him warily, aware I'd never been in a situation quite like this one. While studying at the academy, there were many times when I thought I was in love with one of the handsome mages. Catching their attention brought excitement, but deep inside was an understanding that mages went to their postings and rarely married. It was allowed yet not encouraged.

Protectors focused on the task at hand, for developing romantic relationships led to tension and potential vulnerabilities. Distance might drive the couple apart, too, for mages were sent to postings that complemented their abilities and there were no guarantees that couples would be placed together.

For once, I didn't hide my feelings as I let my gaze linger on Rhyme. The compelling power in his bare shoulders, the feel of his long hands when he touched me, the fall of his dark hair, and the black lines of a tattoo that swirled up one arm. A warmth of awareness filled me. Instead of speaking, I waited for him to continue.

"I would like to take you to my home. Would that be agreeable to you?"

"I thought this was your home."

"It is. As long as I work for my uncle. When I was young, I promised my uncle, Lord Edwin, fifteen years of service. I thought it was what I wanted. Turns out I was wrong, but I've always had a home in the lowlands, near the coast, waiting for my return."

"By the water," I breathed, thinking of how it would complement my magic.

"Yes. It is clear that staying here in the mountain, although a secure defensive place, also comes with hidden dangers for both of us. We don't know who was in the monster's lair, but a continued investigation will be difficult if they find you first."

I nodded. "I've been thinking of that. Whoever it was had the opportunity to kill us when we were healing. Why not strike with a blade? Why use poison?"

"Exactly. I considered that myself. I believe the intent was to look normal. A bloody death would draw attention."

"So does a monster stealing women, and strange runes left behind."

"Whoever is behind this wants us to believe the monster is dead so our worries are assuaged. Phera, don't take this the wrong way. I'm aware it's only been a few days, but there have been no incidents so far. What makes you believe someone else was there in the caves?"

I stiffened. So he didn't believe me. "There's more I haven't told you."

His face darkened as I told him about the mysterious person who'd blindfolded me and demanded answers with a knife.

When I finished, he shook his head, jaw tight. "Why didn't you tell me?"

"I couldn't be sure who my enemies were."

A tense silence stretched between us, our unsaid thoughts so loud I almost felt the hum of them.

At last, he sighed. "Fair enough. I wasn't sure if my bride would slay me with magic."

A laugh burst from my lips, breaking the tension of the moment. "To slay an ice lord? Here, in the vast mountain where I'm gravely outnumbered?"

Instead of smiling, he scowled. "Yes, even though killing an ice lord goes against the rules of the Academy of Mages, there's always the possibility. The wildness out here makes people do strange things. Besides, my people are terrified of mages, of magic ruling our lives. One mage is worth one hundred warriors."

My eyebrows rose. "Mages are only as powerful as the group of people we work with. Usually a group of five is chosen to protect a city, and that combines a healer, two to three mages with various skills, offensive and defensive, and a couple of warriors. The combination of minds, of cleverness, and brute strength. Which is why working with you, Lord Isak, and Lessie is preferable. Together, we can do more to investigate and stop this growing evil."

"As I've seen." Rhyme folded his arms across his chest, his jaw set as he stared out the window. "I'm just curious why *my* clan was targeted."

I frowned. "Earlier, you said the other clans were attacked."

"Attacked, yes, but they didn't have mysterious disappearances. I talked to Lord Edwin, and he said some curious things. Tomorrow, if you're up to it, I want to take you to see the seer. Perhaps she has something to do with this."

"There's a seer? Here? Isn't that too akin to magic?"

"She tells the future and so she was allowed to live, and she has no connection to the past bloodlines of mages."

My mouth fell open, my thoughts racing. This was the first time he'd alluded to mages being in the north. "This makes no sense."

"Perhaps it was a mistake. But we shall see. We shall leave tomorrow, and when we return, we'll go directly to my home."

A shy smile came to my lips, and I dropped my gaze. "I'd like that."

Leaning forward, Rhyme took my hand. "Phera, this is new for me too. Marriages are serious here. It's a bond of honor and respect, a promise to each other, a sacred covenant that cannot be broken. We've heard of how marriages are treated in the southern lands, as something that can be as easily broken as a piece of string. That's not how we treat each other here, and I meant every word of the vows I spoke. I'm sorry for my part in the lies you were told and the feelings of betrayal you carry. I wanted no part of it, but I also felt a duty to protect my people. But you are my wife. I should protect you first."

"Rhyme, let's put it in the past, and promise to work together with transparency and honesty."

"I vow to be honest with you, to honor and respect you, to treat you as my equal, and to protect you from the suspicions my people carry."

I took his calloused hand in both of mine, feeling the roughness of his palm. A man's hand. A warrior's hand. "Rhyme. I vow to be honest with you. To honor and respect you. To treat you as my equal, and to protect you from the wildness of magic. I want to help. I want to be here."

"I know," he said. "I want you here. I want you to help."

Then he leaned across the bed and swept me into

his lap. His hands threaded into my hair while I wrapped my arms around his shoulders, enjoying the steadiness, the strength of him. My lips were already parted when he brushed his across mine, the kiss I'd longed for consuming me, awakening a fire within. I kissed him back, a heartbeat of passion tumbling free.

He held me close, kissing me slowly, tenderly, as though we had to make up for lost time. With each kiss, each touch, a fever of heat came over me until it wasn't enough. I wanted him to consume me with all of his being.

His hands came around my waist, pulling the shawl off my shoulders. He lay me back, and I gripped his shoulders, keeping us skin to skin. We kissed as his fingers slid up my dress. I lifted my hips, letting him settle between my legs. Using my mouth, my breath, my hands, I urged him on, and we moved in a rhythm of slow kisses, pounding pulses, and fiery passion.

I was his, and he was mine. And the euphoria that consumed me was better than the buzz of pleasure magic gave me. It was intoxicating and all-consuming, and best of all, it was pure and uncorrupted. It was as beautiful as a snowy day, as hot as a burning fire, and when it was over, tears of joy slid down my cheeks.

At last, I felt forgiven and complete.

# Phera

The seer lived in the hills, between the lowlands and the mountains. Rhyme and I took the yaks—who'd made it safely back from the incident with the shadow cats—laden with supplies, as though we were going on a long journey. We'd left before dawn, wearing long cloaks to hide our identities.

Isak and Lessie came to the stables where the yaks were kept to see us off. I didn't like the omen in the air, the idea of being separated again, for that was when harm struck. Lessie encouraged me, agreeing that the seer might be a piece to the puzzle, and while she was too weak to travel far, Rhyme and I might stumble on some semblance of truth.

I kept thinking how foolish it was, because if the seer

was involved, she'd attack. Rhyme and I might not be enough to take her down. Or perhaps it was fear, because I didn't have another mage to back me up and I felt like I was on the edge of a discovery.

We traveled past the outpost and on for a while. Once the sea curved away, we turned inland and traveled into the wood. Deer bounded away as we passed and icicles hung off the trees like decoration. I shivered in my heavy furs, more from apprehension than with cold. For comfort, I rubbed Rosie's thick fur, grateful for her presence. She was solid and large, and those horns, if swung in the right direction, would do some damage.

Rhyme came to a stop by a path leading upward. "We walk from here," he said, dismounting.

With a nod, I swung my leg over Rosie's back. She was already nudging a snow drift. "Will they stay right here?" I asked, eyeing the free-roaming yaks.

Rhyme pushed the hood of his furred cloak back, then approached me. One hand rested on my hip and I did not understand why the power of his presence calmed me, but it did. My soul sang and a peace filled me. I leaned into him, enjoying his solid strength and the clarity that had passed between us. There was something else, though. My magic—it hummed stronger than before.

"The yaks will stay right here," Rhyme confirmed.

"We don't have to do this if you don't want to. I can go alone."

There it was, the iron resolve within me. I wanted to find out what was terrorizing the ice people, who'd wanted me to become a sacrifice to the monster, and who'd drained Lessie's blood. Whoever it was, it was pure evil. I wouldn't back away from stopping them.

Sliding my good hand into Rhyme's, I squeezed. "I'm ready."

Snowflakes drifted out of the sky as we followed the zigzagging path up the hill toward the summit. The trek was strenuous, but Rhyme stopped from time to time, giving me a moment to catch my breath. Walking pulled on my still-healing wounds, and at some point, I wondered if the delicate skin had ripped and started bleeding again, but the pain remained dull. Besides, I wanted answers. My discomfort wouldn't make me turn back.

The path ended at the summit where a rock wall rose. Around the bend was the entrance to a cave, and I shuddered, my thoughts returning to the horror of the monster's lair.

I shrugged my furs closer while Rhyme put up a hand, bringing us to a halt. He took a flask out of his pocket and unscrewed it, offering it to me first. "You'll want this."

No questions asked, I took a sip of the liquid and let the burn of the brandy warm me up. I handed it back and Rhyme took a quick sip, wiped his mouth, then tapped the flask against the stone. It rang out like a door knocker and I hugged my arms around myself, waiting.

A thin, reedy voice called, "Your arrival was foretold this morning. Do two warriors stand at my doorstep, seeking knowledge about the future?"

*Rhyme was the warrior but I was a protector, why would she call us both warriors?*

"We do," Rhyme responded.

I stayed rigid, my voice locked in my throat. A seer. What if she could divine my past and convinced Rhyme that I belonged in a dungeon, not here?

"Why come to me? What is so dire that you seek my help?"

Rhyme shifted his weight from one foot to the other, his grip tight on the handle of his axe. "It is a long tale, and I am hesitant to speak without knowing where your allegiance lies."

Silence followed.

Then a shadow fell across the path and a shriveled old woman appeared. Furs swallowed her tiny body, and her brown skin was so wrinkled it sagged over her fragile bones. Claw-like fingers curved around her neck, holding her furs shut, and the whites of her eyes stared at us. She was blind, like Mage Margot.

The fragrant scent of tobacco drifted to my nose, drawing my attention to the long pipe she carried in her other hand. Taking a long drag, she blew out a series of smoke rings. They floated above our heads, disappearing into the snow.

Cocking her head as though she were examining us, she took another drag, then waved her clawed hand. "Curious. Very curious indeed. I expected two warriors, but before me stands an ice lord and a mage. Since when did ice lords forget their oath and allow mages to enter their midst?"

"A new era has come," Rhyme said.

The seer hummed deep in her throat but said nothing else.

We followed her around the bend into her maw. A nest of branches served as a gate which covered the entrance of the cave. It had been pushed aside when she exited and she left it open, despite the chill winds that blew in from the elevation.

A flameless fire smoked near the entrance and she huddled beside it, muttering words under her breath. I caught some of them and assumed she was speaking in another tongue. It left me feeling uncomfortable, and I lingered at the entrance, doubting this plan.

Seers believed in higher power, in faith, and in divining the future from dreams, visions, premonitions, and even the constellation of stars. Their powers, like magic, could not necessarily be learned and were graced upon an individual. I'd never had the pleasure of meeting a seer, nor did I want to.

"Tell me what ails you," the seer said. Then she pointed her pipe at Rhyme. "Not you, her."

My voice cracked as I spoke. "Nothing ails me."

More muttering. "When you're ready to stop telling lies, come back. Otherwise, you're wasting my time."

I felt Rhyme's gaze shift to me, waiting for me to speak up, to offer something to the seer. I fumbled with the words, turning them over in my mind until I landed on a question. "Do you know what has happened to the women of the clan?"

"There are many clans. You'll have to be more specific."

Many. It occurred to me that I didn't know the name of Rhyme's clan.

"My clan," Rhyme spoke up. "We dwell in Eyre Heights, by the sea."

"Lord Edwin's clan," the seer confirmed, shifting away from us. "Aye. I know that clan. They were the ones who instigated the mage massacres."

I stiffened. Massacres? Rhyme hadn't told me about this. Suddenly, I found it hard to breathe.

"It was over two hundred years ago," Rhyme stated, voice hard.

So he knew and he was ashamed. It was a secret he'd kept from me, with good reason. What else was he hiding?

"Time matters not if the heart hasn't changed."

Anger made me speak up. "You haven't answered my question. Instead, you make accusations, seeking to divide us with distractions."

This time, the seer's cloud of smoke drifted toward me. "It is because the past is the key to the future. As for your question, yes, I have heard of the strange disappearances."

"Did you have anything to do with them? Are you working with those responsible?"

The seer took a slow drag, mulling over my question. "It is a valid question. I am an outsider, am I not? I don't dwell within the safety of the clans. I've created my mountain of safety here. Suspicion is always cast first on the outsiders. I might be insulted if it wasn't what I would do, were I in your place. Search for answers. But there's another reason you came to me, isn't there, to see if I was responsible, and if not, so I could point a finger and say who is."

Rhyme crossed his arms, his stance still rigid, ready. "Are you pointing the finger at yourself or someone else?"

"Long have I waited for your arrival. Long have I sat here, holding my visions close. But instead of coming to me, your chieftain sent for mages. Now that was a very curious action. I asked myself, why? Why not visit the seer? Because she is an outsider and untrustworthy? Or because she could see through the plans of those responsible and point the finger at the right person? Or perhaps they forgot. It's always assumed that the loneliness and the cold or the wildness we live on the cusp of will break in and slay me. Better for an ice warrior to seal my doom than for nature to take its course. But no one asked me. They forgot, and in forgetting, they made a grave mistake."

My throat went dry, and I wished for another sip of brandy. The truth swam so close, yet held back by the grasping fingers of the seer. I wanted her to speak faster, to reveal all, but it was not her way. She wanted to speak slowly, in circles, letting us speculate about the truth. I wondered if she also intended to turn us on each other. Words rose, but I forced them down, remaining silent, giving her time to speak.

The seer reached out a hand. It shook as she picked up a stick and started drawing in the ash around the fire.

"Let us suppose that someone from the bloodline of massacred mages survived. Let us assume they faded into society, living a normal life, forgetting about magic, until magic forgot about them. As the decades passed, their family line took on a new name, while the old vanished into legend. All would have gone on as usual, except for one fact. Magic is wild and unruly, and while it occasionally runs through bloodlines, it can skip entire generations. Then someone will have a spark and magic will ignite. If one lives on the edges of the unknown lands, where magic has a tendency to pull out the darkness in mages, then it would be no different."

"But magic has to be taught," I interrupted. "One doesn't simply *know* magic instinctively."

The seer lifted her stick, disliking the interruption. "Ah, a mage from the southern lands, taught magic, instructed in the way to use it to avoid darkness and devastation. But it is instinctive, isn't it? Who taught you how to use dark magic, blood magic? Is it not forbidden, yet you used it anyway?"

I pressed my lips together, wishing I hadn't spoken up.

"Do you speak in truth or hyperbole?" Rhyme asked.

"Do you know why blood magic, specifically, is forbidden? Because life is in the blood, and taking a life leads to darkness. Blood, though, *is* magic, and if one has enough of it, the possibilities are endless. One could raise an army, create portals, control monsters. If one has blood, one has ultimate power. Even more so if it is magical blood, and that is a secret the mages of the academy surely don't want anyone to know. Blood magic is the most powerful magic. With it, one can control souls. One could devastate the world."

A tightness filled my chest. My fingers itched as an acute awareness filled me. I just needed to reach out, to trail my fingers along the dirty wall, to sink them into the ash from previous fires, to roam across her belongings. The truth was right in front of me, I just needed to touch it in order to know.

Stepping a few more paces into the cave, I let the strong odors that lay there swallow me whole, and then I placed the flat of my palm against the wall. My sprained wrist burned, but I ignored the pain. A blur of bright colors filled the edges of my vision and a voice came from somewhere, whether in my head or outside of it, I wasn't sure. A weight settled on my shoulders, so heavy I bent over, and understanding filled me.

Long ago, there had been a war between the ice warriors and the mages. The mages stole them for blood sacrifice, and so the ice warriors struck back with the blade. It was a brutal, nasty fight, and likely where the tales of ice lords being savages came from. One would assume that powerful magic would win against any blade, but the ice lords had something the mages did not expect. The mages' energy was drained, and one by one, they fell.

The vision ended and I returned to the cave, eyes glassy, the weight pressing hard against me. What the seer had drawn in the ash was clear to see now. It was Eyre Heights, the mountain, the outpost with the flying beasts and the sea, a wave churning closer.

She stayed hunched over, eyes closed, the pipe smoke fading. "So the mage has a bit of seer in her. She can see visions too."

Her words surprised me, but she was right. Knowledge that hadn't been my own came to me, and the burden sat heavy on my shoulders.

I pivoted to Rhyme, because despite him being an ice lord, he hadn't been there over two hundred years ago. He was different from those ice warriors and I had to remember that. When I looked at him, I couldn't focus on a past full of death. I had to focus on what the future might be. Our future. Long ago, ice warriors and mages had been at odds, but this was an opportunity to be at peace, but only if it was done right. Oh, but the truth made it much harder.

"It's the mountain," I said. "We have to go back."

# Phera

The seer required payment in goods, food, water, and a sack of coins. Rhyme, thankfully, had planned ahead and swung down the sack he carried on his back. We waited while the seer felt through it, her face wrinkling even further as she lifted and smelled each item before replacing it. The snow had picked up when we ducked back outside, and Rhyme's hand rested on my back, drawing me toward him. I stiffened, reminded of what the seer had revealed.

He bent his dark head, his words coaxing, softening the sharp edges of my anger. "Don't hold the past of my people against me."

"Why didn't you tell me?"

"I did not deem it relevant, and the truth of the matter is, what was done back then was an act of war and of fear. It is not something that is spoken of, partially because it was so gruesome, and I also believe the warriors of that time did what they believed needed to be done. War is evil and there are drastic actions of wrongdoing that take place on either side. Mage against man and man against mage, except in this age, in this time, we have the opportunity to work together."

I spun to face him. "Except that's not quite what's happening. Back in there, I saw a vision. The seer was right. Someone from the bloodline survived and they've been clever, waiting, planning, biding their time, and now they've struck. Your clan is being haunted by a mage. So where does that leave us?"

Rhyme sighed. "The burden I carry is never easy. Phera, this knowledge changes nothing between us. You are still you—a beautiful, powerful mage, strong and clever, with a good heart. And I am an ice lord, —a warrior, a protector. Together, we can stop this menace, but I need your help, your trust, and you need mine. Are you willing?"

I came to a standstill on the path, snow melting in my hair, and stared up at my husband. There was something eternally beautiful about him, standing in the wild, the snow swirling around him, furs covering his powerful shoulders, and a question in those dark eyes. A longing swelled in my heart and my throat went thick. I was curious about what the future held for us and I wanted it almost as much as I'd wanted to become a mage. Our future lay like an eggshell, fragile and in danger of shattering unless it was protected, and I had the power to do so. All I needed to do was step forward and leave behind the knowledge of the past. It was dead and gone, and he was right—transgressions had been made on either side, and those who made them were to be held responsible for their actions in the afterlife.

But I had the power to change my present and guide my future, not by making the same mistakes of the past, but by making a focused effort to shift and change. If I didn't take a step forward in crossing the bridge between ice warrior and mage—into turning what had been a war in the past to a blooming partnership in the future—who would?

There would always be evil in the world. Some of it might come from men, from ice warriors, from monsters, from the beyond. And some evil might rise directly from the Academy of Mages, from people with magic I respected and learned from. There weren't sides of right or good or evil, there was only now, me and him, and what we would do.

Trust and honesty were the first steps. It was the beginning, and such a beginning I would have.

Holding out my hand, I stepped forward. "I am willing."

In response, he kissed me. It wasn't the tentative kiss of newly married strangers, as we'd been on our wedding day. It wasn't the kiss of last night, when at last we saw eye to eye. It was gentle and sweet, and it felt like arriving home. This kiss carried a promise, to honor and trust each other, to work together to protect each other's interests. Yet it was more, much more than that too. It was the kiss that foreshadowed love, a dark attraction, a deepening desire. Parting my lips, I let his warmth swallow me whole.

Time ebbed away, and when, instead of releasing me, the circle of his arms tightened around my waist, I leaned in, hungry for more. The intoxication of his lips, the feel of his hard body pressing against mine, the safety of his arms, the smell of pine and snow and the sound he made, deep in his throat that matched my own. A longing, a contentment, an arriving.

My eyes were wet when he finally released me and we stood for but a moment to catch our breaths.

Rhyme sighed. "I want nothing more than to leave now and take you away from here."

I shook my head. "We can't, because we are protectors who solve problems, not run from them."

"I had a sense all along that this would be difficult to face."

"Because it's personal. It's happening *to* you, while it's different for me. I feel desperate leaving Lessie in danger, knowing that the only reason she came here was because of me. She had a choice. She shouldn't have come."

"I disagree. Even though it has been dark and dangerous, Isak loves her with his whole being. I'm not sure how or why it happened so quickly, but if anything happens to her, he will not rest."

A smile came to my lips, because for once when I thought of Lessie and Isak, I was no longer jealous of what they had. For the longest time, I'd compared myself to Lessie, but that wasn't acceptable. I wasn't her and she wasn't me. Why should I expect that our lives be similar? She found love instantly, but I had Rhyme.

Our marriage hadn't been a blissful time of love thus far, but we would get there, and there was nothing wrong with two stories taking separate paths. I had to stop comparing my life's story to Lessie's and stop expecting that everything good that happened to her would also happen to me. And neither should she.

Rhyme released me and we returned to the yaks, riding them through the snow back toward Eyre Heights. The wind howled around us and magic swirled within, awakening, answering to the snow. There was so much moisture in the air, my body hummed with the sound of it. I felt strong, alive, waiting to snatch magic out of the air and use it. Anything felt possible on the edges of the wild land, as though a vortex were building.

"Rhyme, when we were with the seer, I had a vision. I saw not only the decimation of the mages and the horrors of the past, but I also saw the future. I wondered for a time why the seer was alive, and why she would survive if someone with magic wanted to destroy the clans. If anything, the seer should be killed first, that she might not reveal the plans of that individual."

"I've wondered that myself. Why *does* the seer live? The clans will not take it upon themselves to shed innocent blood. At least, not of humankind. She is harmless and has shown no hostilities toward us."

"I believe that was her intent all along, because she's part of the madness happening here."

Rhyme swore. "She made no indication."

"No, nor did she have to. I wondered myself if she knew of my gift. I honestly didn't think of it myself. But perhaps I've gained the abilities of a seer. It is a more recent awakening within me. I've known magic, but in the past few weeks, I've had visions like none I've ever had before."

"Is it the union?"

"What do you mean?"

"Remember, in ancient days, the union of a mage and magic-less human were powerful, because the blood covenant unlocked the full powers of a mage."

An awareness came over me. That first night after we married, Rhyme and I had been together and ever since then, I had felt a shift. Yet the visions had come before. Was it possible that a union with him gave me access to my full power? I'd attributed my ability to stop the monster to blood magic and pure panic, but perhaps it was much more than that.

"I wonder why the academy kept that knowledge from the mages. In truth, in the southern lands, mages do not marry."

"Why not?"

"Our lives are given wholly to the protection of others. Love and families are a distraction. I should have told you the truth sooner, but mages are usually barren."

"Usually?" Rhyme echoed, his voice hollow.

"It is rare that a mage will have children."

"But it is also rare that they marry."

I weighed my thoughts before responding. "I suspect that the southern lands are afraid of magic, of the wildness, the chaos it brings. I wonder how many know the legends of what happened here in the northern lands, and quashed that story. Magic is strictly regulated in the southern lands, and if one steps out of line, they are banished to the dungeons."

"Or sent here to marry a savage ice lord?" Rhyme pointed out. His lips quirked back in a half smile.

I rubbed the back of my neck, face burning. "Or that."

He had a way of lightening the air despite the seriousness of our conversation. "Ah, but I interrupted. You were saying something about the seer, how she is still alive, yes, but also she is part of it. Should we go back?"

"No, we need to return to the mountain and find Renava. I believe she is the one we've been looking for, the legacy child of the mages, the one with latent powers who awoke. She's been careful, very careful, but she didn't plan on Lessie and I living. Nor did she plan on us going to the seer or my power to see visions to awaken."

Rhyme shook his head. "Renava is a warrior, a hunter. She's quiet and keeps to herself but. . .it's difficult to believe that she would have plans for revenge."

"I'm trying not to assume, but I heard her voice, and when Lessie was captured, it was a woman with dark hair who bent over the rock, holding a knife. The only woman out there was Renava. I believe I saw her in my vision. If we can capture her and ask, we will discover what her plans are."

"And what is it you believe she intends to do?"

"Eyre Heights is a haven, a mountain that blocks the effects of magic. Mages cannot use their power to the full extent in the mountain, and so it is impossible to take it with magic."

"I didn't know that," Rhyme said.

"I noticed little things, but it wasn't until we left the mountain that I realized that it naturally suppresses magic. Others might have magic, too, but they haven't noticed. But I believe she will take the bones and blood and raise them up to become an army that will attack."

"This sounds outlandish. Impossible."

I nodded gravely, trying to see from his perspective. "It does. It is what I saw in the vision, though. . .an impossible force crushing the mountain. How would that be possible without an army?"

Rhyme made a low sound in his throat. "An army that will take warriors to vanquish."

"Both warriors and mages—there will be no sides this time. We will have to fight together."

# Phera

The sky was gray. Waves roared, rolling onto the coast, warning of an approaching storm. I felt like the waters—restless, irritated, the visions flashing through my mind.

We left the yaks in the stable, where I spent extra time patting Rosie's head and feeding her carrots. I went directly to Lessie with what I'd learned, while Rhyme and Isak went to find Renava. Rhyme said that Renava would be more receptive to warriors, but I wondered if she would even bother to show her hand in front of them.

Lessie was up, fully dressed, hair braided.

"You must feel better," I exclaimed.

She smiled. "Yes, I feel renewed. What came of going to see the seer?"

I told her about my visions and of the past war between ice lords and mages, how they were all vanquished and only the seer remained, but it was likely she was playing both sides.

Lessie was quiet, thoughtful as tears sprung to her eyes. She wiped them away with the back of her hand and took a deep breath. "No one said this would be easy, but it hurts my heart to think of the past, and to think of what might come for these people in the future. If it is, indeed, Renava, we have to stop her."

"I think we are all in agreement there. It's the how..."

Lessie held up her hand. "Isak and Lord Rhyme are looking for her, but we have to assume that once we left the house of healing, it's likely she fled to focus on her plans. It's clear that while our deaths were preferred, they didn't change her plans. If she fled, where would it be? Back to the monster's lair?"

I shook my head. "No, it was far away. It would take days to travel to it."

"Unless she used a portal."

"But would she want to exhaust her magic like that right before unleashing chaos?" I countered.

"If she wanted to lie low, it would make sense."

"What if she had another place to go? Lord Rhyme mentioned a home, and so did Isak, somewhere outside of this mountain. He told me the people used to live in the lowlands before they became too dangerous. Now they only live there during the summer months, when all is calm. The other clans came to an alliance, but the chieftains change, and the whims of each clan also change. There are also bandits, roving tribes of outlaws here who dwell on the outskirts. Not to mention the dangers of the unknown lands," I added.

Lessie nodded. "You said the seer lives in a cave a short walk from here."

"An hour or two by yak."

"Did you see anything else up there?"

I frowned. I'd been in pain and nervous about what the seer might reveal so I'd paid little attention to my surroundings and I'd trusted Rhyme to guide me. "It's possible there are other caves, tunnels that connect. Like you said, the ice lords didn't always live in the mountain and it sounded like the mages dwelled in the forests and caves, not in the lowlands. At least, not during the war. What if she found an old place, much like the monster's lair, and decided to dwell there?"

Lessie closed her eyes. "We need to leave this mountain and search for her."

Renava, indeed, had fled, and we searched for her for two days, to no avail. Rhyme spoke of the hidden places in the mountain and Lessie and I brainstormed together.

Meanwhile, the ice people mourned for those whose lives had been stolen, and a blanket of sorrow enveloped Eyre Heights. The interest in Lessie and I had faded, the mages who had stopped the disappearance, but each morning, I woke to the quickness of my pulse, with the knowledge that time was running out.

# Rhyme

It was the silence of waiting that made me restless. I prowled the edges of Eyre Heights, scanned the skies, and alerted my warriors. Then finally, unable to make any headway, I went to see Lord Edwin. This time, I went to his private chambers. Not that a private meeting would cool his attitude toward me. The door jerked open on the first rap of my knuckles, and Lord Edwin towered above me, scowling. "I thought you left."

I pushed inside, shutting the door behind me. "I went to see the seer."

"Now you're engaging in sorcery?"

"The mages are right. Something else *is* coming for us. The disappearances, the slaying of our clanswomen —it's only the beginning."

Lord Edwin strode to the fire and crossed his arms, a scowl darkening his face. "I'm listening."

And that was why Lord Edwin was the chieftain. He might be a hard man, brutal and shrewd in his ways, but he listened to reason.

"It is thought that the seer is working with someone here, someone who has latent magical powers and will use them against us to raise an army to slay the ice lords, as the mages were slain long ago." I paused, but Lord Edwin didn't flinch. So I asked the question I should have asked a few days ago. "Where is Renava? Was she the one who persuaded you to bring in the mages?"

At first, he froze, and then his face went ashen. "It's her, isn't it?"

"Where is she now?" I demanded.

"I don't know. I haven't seen her for days."

"Uncle, she's planning something. I fear it is evil."

He swore. "I know it is evil."

"How?"

"If you breathe a word of this to anyone, I will have your head. She's been my mistress the past year."

"You have no intentions of marrying her?"

"No, she is not the right material to be a chieftain's wife. My refusal disappointed her."

"The night of the disappearances, can you recall where she was? Was she with you?"

"I sleep heavily, so I wouldn't know if she left and returned."

I crossed my arms, a fury rising. Mages were the source of our problems, yet they were also our solution. Odd, though, that Renava wouldn't recruit Lady Lessie and Phera to work with her. Instead, she used them for her own plans. "Where would she be hiding?"

"There is a lookout above the mountain. I haven't been there in ages. It's old, falling into disuse. Look for her there."

"Whatever she has planned is here, for this mountain. The people need to leave."

"Leave and go where? A storm is setting in."

"Anywhere is safer than here."

# Phera

The wind was cutting as we made our way up the slope toward the old outpost. The path went past the stables where the yaks had been turned loose, and zigzagged up the mountainside. Snowfall was much deeper up there and I struggled along in my boots, each step making my feet sink up to my calves. Holding my furs around my neck with my good hand, I held the other out, ready to summon magic.

While the outpost was invisible from down below, Rhyme and Isak knew the way, and Lessie had insisted she was well enough to come. But whoever or whatever was up there would see us coming and could rain down magic, set a trap, or pepper us with arrows before we arrived. Hence, Lessie went first, holding up her shield of magic, a bluish aura that arched over us like an umbrella.

One more zigzag and the first arrow came, whining through the wind, then slashing into the magical barrier Lessie held, right where her heart would be. Another came quickly, then three more. Isak stepped back to nock an arrow in his bow, but Rhyme shook his head. "It's no use. We can't see from this angle. That was the point of the outpost—no one can reach it without being destroyed first."

We kept pushing until the ground evened out and a cave appeared, or at least, what had originally been a cave. A hollowed opening arched, but doors had been built in. Above was the tower, three stories high, and it was from there those arrows came.

"I suppose the keep is locked," Isak called out.

"Stand back," I called to them, moving to stand behind Lessie. I summoned the snow, forming it into a ball, hard and compacted together. Hefting the snow, I imagined the doors shattering and splintering. I released, and a swish buzzed past my ears as the ball smashed into the doors. An eerie cracking came before splintering wood caved in.

Rhyme and Isak rushed forward while Lessie and I followed. Lessie sagged against the doorway, letting the shield drop. Sweat beaded on her forehead and her breath came in shallow pants.

I patted her shoulder. "Sit, rest."

"You'll need me," she protested.

"You need to regain your energy. It's no good if you're too exhausted to fight."

Lessie covered my hand with her own. "You don't know, do you?"

"Know what?"

"What gives a mage bride strength?"

Now was hardly the time for this kind of discussion. I anxiously cast my eyes across the place. It was desolate and dusty, but a clear path led across the hall to the next set of stairs. "What gives a mage bride strength?" I asked, trying to keep the impatience out of my tone.

"Her husband—her mortal, non-magical husband," Lessie clarified.

A mix of surprise and discomfort overcame me as understanding sunk in.

Isak was by her side in an instant and swept her into his arms. I glanced away, unable to watch the intimate moment they shared.

Apparently unbothered by it all, Rhyme nodded to me. "Phera?"

I pointed toward the stairs and we went up, moving as

silently as we could. Above us, we heard nothing but silence, making my heart beat faster. When we reached the first landing, Isak and Lessie joined us, and I had to admit, Lessie looked much better. Her eyes were bright, shoulders tall, and there was a freshness to her appearance. Was it possible that love had such an effect on magic?

We moved on up to the next landing, which was, again, silent.

On the third floor, the tension in the air thickened to something tangible. The scent of iron and blood came, along with a wild magic. The stench of it filled my nostrils. Wild magic. Corrupt magic. Evil magic. I'd smelled a hint of it before. That day when the bridge collapsed, it was because of magic.

What a difference there was between good and evil. Now I had clarification on why the Academy of Mages had judged me so harshly. It was because once someone gave in to magic, the harshness of it, the wildness of it, the beginning of chaos, it became easier to do it over and over again. No matter what happened, I could never use blood magic again. There had to be another way or how would I be different from Renava, seeking revenge?

We burst onto the third floor, shattering barriers as though they were nothing, and there she stood, alone. There was no army, no bones, no death and devastation. Only Renava, looking much like she did when we'd gone hunting together. She lifted her bow, and even before she shot, I saw she was out of arrows.

"That's enough," Rhyme said, and her shoulders sagged. "Why are you shooting at us? We've been nothing but your friends, your allies."

A grim smile came to her lips. "I think you know why. You've come all this way to foil my plans, but you're too late."

"What do you mean?" Rhyme snapped, edging toward her. "I know you tricked my uncle, pretending to be his mistress while whispering poison into his ear, telling him to bring mages here that you could use for your own purposes."

Renava blanched. "You wouldn't believe me if I told you I actually loved him, but he was easy to manipulate and strangers are much easier to kill than friends. I did what I had to do. I took enough blood to raise a foe that you will not defeat, not even with the mages. My life doesn't matter anymore. So go ahead, slay me if that's what you've come to do. Your doom has been sealed. I've made sure of that."

"But why?" I interrupted. "Why do you want to see the demise of the clan?"

Her eyes narrowed and her voice came low and harsh, a whispered tone I recognized from when she'd blindfolded and knifed me. "They killed my people, turned me into an oddity, forced me to hide in my own home. Worst, they got away with it. But perhaps it was time. There's always something or someone stronger, more powerful, who can take the place of others. Mages, for all their magic, weren't strong enough to defeat ice warriors, and thus their era ended. Now it's time for the end of the ice warriors, to give the land back to the wild. So go ahead, I've opened the door and I've let the monster in. There's nothing you can do to me now to stop it."

"Renava, you're a mage, like Phera and I," Lessie pleaded. "We could have helped you."

"You? You're weak. I saw your arrival in the clouds and listened to your conversations. You're the kind who are afraid to get your hands dirty, afraid to use wild magic, and afraid to do whatever it takes. I know your tales. Lessie, how you were bullied at your posting until you left, and Phera, you had such potential, a criminal who should be in the dungeons. But even you disappointed me. I've learned that you can't rely on anyone if you have plans to achieve. You must go your own way, use those whom you can, and that's exactly what I've done. Nothing against any of you, but it's time. I only regret that my name won't be recorded in the history books, or that if you kill me now, I won't be able to see what I've wrought."

"And what have you wrought?" Isak demanded, blade out.

"I've used blood magic in all its forms. Blood magic is pure and strong, but it was the blood of a mage that I really needed, for that blood is potent. Watch with me. Here comes the storm."

The storm. It had been needling at me, thrusting and alive, awake with power and I felt it now, a storm impending, coming toward us, leaping, chasing. The thunder on the horizon, the lightning flash, and the darkness as the sun and moon set on a course to collide. Fear made my skin tingle, and I reached into my pocket, fingering the magical bracelets I'd intended to toss away.

With a glance at Lessie, we rushed her. Magic poured in golden waves from her palms, but she was no match for Lessie's shield, nor my water magic, which hurled her to the floor. I was upon her in a second, snapping the magical bracelets around her wrists. She spat at me, bucking up, but I released her and stepped back, facing Rhyme and Isak. "Her magic is suppressed, but it is not up to us to bring judgment or to slay her. She should have a jury of peers, in accordance with the laws of the Academy of Mages. They shall hear of her deeds, judge her and decide her fate."

"It's much too late for that," she spat, and was on her feet in a moment.

It happened so quickly, I had no recourse. One moment she was standing, the next she was hurling her body out the window. There came a sickening crack, then silence. My stomach churned and bile rose in my throat.

Lessie gave a cry and hurled herself into Isak's chest.

Rhyme's hand landed on my shoulder and he drew me to himself, face grim. "We have to see what the storm brings."

A slight tremor came, and the stone beneath my feet groaned, as though it were alive. Next came a rumble, then ear-shattering cracking sounds. Dust rained down from the rafters, and suddenly, Rhyme's hand was on my arm. "Run!" he shouted, urging us all toward the stairs.

I threw my arms out to keep my balance as I ran. I'd heard of earthquakes, terrible disasters that ripped the land in half, opening up holes in the ground and swallowing others whole. I never imagined I'd experience one myself, and the fear that gripped my heart made it difficult to breathe.

Somehow, we stumbled our way out of the tower, but the shaking on the mountain was worse. I fell to my knees, jarring my sprained wrist. One brutal truth floated to the surface of my mind: in the grip of nature, magic would not save me.

# Rhyme

Snow filled the air, blowing into my ears and mouth and nose, sticking to the edges of my beard. I lifted my hand and shielded my eyes, blinking against the driving force. Ominous black clouds hovered, and what daylight there had been when we'd reached the tower was steadily fading. While we were inside interrogating Renava, the sun and moon had come together in the sky, and whatever evil she'd summoned had awakened.

Screams filled my ears as a white wave ripped from the sea and swirled toward the mountain, determined to drown it. But it was what came from the depths that made the blood drain from my face. My legs suddenly felt too weak to hold myself upright and a guttural cry burst from my lips.

Death lay upon us all.

There was no weapon, no force, no magic that could haunt the rise of a sleeping giant. For out of those waves came a white, horse-like nose. A mane of scales, ice-blue orbs for eyes, and an eel-thick body. Except it was no eel but a sea dragon, rising from the depths. It could wrap its body around the mountain, open its great maw, and swallow us all whole.

There were legends of what lay in the sea, tales that no one took seriously because they were fables, an idea of the world in ancient times. No one believed there were actually sea monsters or that a sea dragon could be awoken and rise from the depths. No one believed because no one had seen, but the absence of seeing did not delineate the truth. I was seeing now, and apparently, Renava had believed that with enough sacrifice, enough blood, she could awaken a monster and leave us to our doom. All along, the signs had been pointing toward this large-scale travesty: a portal, a monster, the disappearance of us all.

She'd been patient, she'd planned, she'd waited— and worst of all, she'd succeeded.

I fastened my grip on my axe, eyeing the trembling path. Stones had fallen away, but it was still possible to navigate it, although the danger of falling into the sea had increased. I took a step forward, because it was the only way. Forward into chaos, to fight to save my people from the monster or die trying.

"Wait!"

It was Phera, wide-eyed, wild curls blowing about her face. A grave sadness tugged at my heart as I looked at her. Phera, my mage bride, my wife. The mysterious woman I'd come to care for, the woman I wanted to live a life with. A long life. We'd come together for this moment, yet I wanted it to last longer than a memory, longer than another blight on the ice warriors. In the past, we'd slain mages. Now it was time to live together, in harmony, and that chance was being ripped away.

Her gloved hand closed around my arm. "Do you have a plan?"

"I'm going down there," I said, because it was true. "I am a warrior to my core. I must fight until there is nothing left to fight for."

She nodded, a fierceness in her expression, and I loved her for it. It was her strength that drew me in. "We need a plan. We can't attack heedlessly, not with a monster of that size. I need to get down to the water, but you need to stay back. Use bows and arrows, throw axes if you must, but stay up here where you have the summit. Weapons will be inefficient against it, but it will be enough of a distraction."

The ground beneath my feet shook again as I

cupped her face, drawing her to me. This. I'd longed for this—the softness, the gentleness of a woman, her thoughts, her opinions. I wanted her to live through the day, to live through the monster so I could have her. Entirely. I didn't want to let go, especially when everything was ending.

From day one, I should have ignored my misgivings based on stigmas of the past and trusted her. I should have opened up and loved her. Because mages weren't impure monsters from a time unknown. Mages weren't hellbent on evil. It was something that was taught, as with any human. A gift could be used for good or evil. That was the difference between ice warriors and mages, between humans and monsters.

The rush of emotion that came over me was unusual, but a close encounter with death will change one's perspective.

My throat was tight when I spoke, the words coming out rougher than I intended. "Where will you be?"

"Down by the shoreline. I need to get close. This was why I was called here, to protect your people. But Rhyme. . ." She hesitated, her lips forming my name again in silence. Then her hand was against my cheek and those determined dark eyes held me spellbound. "This will not be our end. I will not believe all this was for naught. I will come back to you. After all we've been through, I've finally started to fall in love with you, to forgive myself for the actions of the past. I will not let evil ruin us nor take us away, and if not in this life, then in the next one, we will find each other. We *will* return to each other."

The ground shook beneath our feet as we held each other, and I felt my heart ripping. At last, there was hope to cling to, but it was all being torn away. Regardless, I had duties to uphold, warriors to assemble, a battle to fight. Time was of the essence, yet it slowed down in her presence. I took those words of hope and held tight to them as I kissed her, long and deep, until I felt her strength, her magic. Perhaps I'd always been able to feel it, a throbbing ocean of emotion, a buzz of power ready to use, and I felt a shift, as though some of it transferred to me.

What was it about loss that made one realize what they actually had all along, yet never had been thankful for?

"Phera, you are a wonder. Your magic is a wonder."

She squeezed my arm. "Keep it distracted. I'll be back."

# Phera

Lessie grabbed my hand, and together, we descended. It was difficult running on moving ground, but whenever we were on the brink of falling down the mountain, Lessie's magic caught us and made straight the path before us. Pellets of hard ice swirled out of the darkened sky, slashing at my face, bruising my skin. Waves crashed against the shore as the sea dragon lifted its long, lizard body out of the waters. Bluish-white scales glistened and a mane of rigid scales ran down its back.

A plan formed in my mind, and even though it was difficult to do two things at once, I gathered my magic, forming it into something bigger, larger than it had ever been. An inkling told me I might need the power of dark magic, but I fought it back. I'd killed twice using dark magic, in desperation to save myself, but I would not give in a third time. There was a reason the mages claimed it led to darkness and corruption, and I would not be part of that.

I would not become like Renava and let myself sink into the madness that claimed many others. If I were to win against the sea dragon, which rose larger than life, spreading impossibly long wings, I'd have to use my magic for good. And nothing else. From what I'd seen at the cave of the seer, it was possible to use light magic to overpower darkness. I just had to reach deep inside myself and give my all. Because within me was a new strength.

I hadn't recognized it until Rhyme kissed me. I felt all of him—his strength, his confidence, his energy, his power. He'd given me a piece of himself and it was that piece I relied on, and the knowledge that I knew exactly what a mage bride was. It meant a partnership between man and mage, a binding of two strengths, an unleashing of might and magic. I gained a piece of him and he gained a piece of me. It made my magic more powerful, and I suspected it made his abilities as a warrior increase. We both benefited from the union, and I no longer felt the draw of darkness, the need to find magic that was outside of my control and use it. I had everything I needed within—all I needed to do was believe.

We reached the shore as the sea dragon unfurled its wings and opened its mouth. It belched a stream of water onto the lowlands, shattering houses, drowning the farmlands with water. But I was too far away. I had to move closer for my plan to be effective. I had to touch the water it touched. Touch it, if possible.

A volley of arrows arched over the mountain and dived into the sea, glancing off the back of the scales. The sea dragon lifted its head toward the mountain and opened its snake-like mouth. A forked tongue came out and a hissing came. Aiming its snout at the mountain, it tilted its head back and prepared for another blast of water.

Lessie came to a stop and her hands went up. Her lips moved in tight concentration and the sky tinted blue as an aura swept between the sea dragon and the mountain of ice warriors. The barrier glowed and the water fell harmlessly back into the sea.

I ran as the dragon thrashed, a froth of water spilling onto the shore. I was up to my ankles, then calves, and finally knees. If I went any further, I'd drown. I put my palms in the water and felt that affinity, that strength. I gathered the threads of it and let it out.

Power roared out of me, threading through the

waters, and I watched in awe as it streaked like a falling star, a blast of white burning brighter and brighter. It slammed into the body of the sea dragon and it rocked backward, falling on its back into the water with a splash. A wave rose, cascading toward me, but I lifted my hand, redirecting it back to whence it had come.

I was under no impression that I'd actually stopped the sea dragon, so I readied another ball of magic. Standing in the water made it much easier. This was what I was born for—to use water magic, to defeat monsters—and that knowledge made it all the easier.

The sea dragon rose, and another ball of magic went out from my hands. It slammed into it again, but this time, its wings went up, countering the blast of water. Magic still struck it, but not as hard. Then the arrows were back, distracting it. The boom of drums came, drowned out by thunder and then a flash of lightning. The storm had arrived and I knew what that meant—if lightning struck water while I was in the sea, I'd sizzle to death in those waves. But I couldn't leave. My battle had just begun.

Magic built within me, and this time, when I released it, a sort of euphoria came over me. The wind and waves, the cold and fear melted away as though I'd ascended to another level of bliss. The sea dragon roared, and the waters swirled around me, trembling from its breath. But nothing could stop me. Nothing could touch me now.

Magic blasted out of me and the tempo increased. Water turned solid beneath my feet, and icy bells rained from my fingertips, turning into shards so sharp they could be swords. I drove the sea dragon back, using all my strength, almost warm from the way magic flowed through me, as though I were a conductor and had tapped into the endless power of magic. Wave after wave soared. The sea moved back, as though I were physically pushing it away from the mountain, away from the ice lords.

As I walked upon the ice, I knew there was only one thing left to do to vanquish the sea dragon once and for all. I lifted my hands and let the magic flow, let it build higher and thicker and deeper than ever before.

Then I closed my eyes and let it flow.

# Rhyme

The warriors were trained well and took up their defensive positions fast. We'd always assumed war would come, not from the sea, but from the land. Regardless, we were ready to defend it. At the first trembling of the mountain, the archers had rushed to their posts and rained arrows down on the sea dragon.

I'd taken my axe and shield, running down to the shore with the warriors trained for hand-to-hand combat. Knowing it was impossible to defeat such a monster, we went anyway, and that's where I watched my bride. Phera.

She was fearless, as the meaning of her name suggested, and the white magic that soared from her fingertips was beautiful. It unfurled like the first snow, twirling through the air, beautiful yet secretly deadly. When it slammed into the sea monster, we all watched in astonishment, daring to believe she might slay it.

But she didn't stop. She kept fighting, and I felt her, felt that power ebb and flow inside of her, growing to something bigger and brighter and stronger. Something deadly and powerful. The water froze beneath her feet and she walked on top of it, calling down the storm and channeling it, using its power to increase her magic.

The sea dragon roared and fought, blasting water, which turned to ice, flapping its wings, but its body was trapped in the water. Phera continued to walk toward it, hurling deathly magic. Lightning flashed around her and she was soaking wet to her core, yet it didn't appear that she felt any of it.

Finally, she lifted her hands. A roar came, not from the sea dragon but from elsewhere, a booming explosion that made the sea rise. A wave swelled and rose as high as the mountain of Eyre Heights. It soared above the head of the sea dragon, then suddenly turned into icy teeth, which slammed into its neck.

It screamed, a terrible sound as the ice pierced it, then dragged it beneath the waves. With a boom, the churning waves settled and the sea froze over.

Phera wavered in place, then collapsed on the ice.

Dropping my shield, I ran down the path, through

the sodden ground to the sea. My feet slipped on the ice and it wasn't until I reached the bank that I realized how far out Phera had pushed the sea dragon.

Gaining my balance, I ran, my throat raw from shouting her name. Everything within me desperately hoped for some kind of miracle. I'd seen what she'd done, the unleashing of pure chaos, and she'd poured her energy, her everything into slaying the monster. It was possible that nothing would be left, just a husk or a shell. Nothing more.

I skidded to a stop beside her prone body and lifted her in my arms. Her clothing was nothing more than slabs of ice clinging to her skin. Her head was back, eyes closed, a look of peace on her face at last. When I lifted her, she was light as a feather, but I felt that pulse, though far away. I might save her. If I ran. Fast.

# Phera

When I opened my eyes, I felt the first inkling of a weather change. Rhyme and I had left the windows open the night before, letting the cool air filter into our home, but now I sensed a new tang in the air—the warm comfort of summer rolling across the sea. I sat up and stretched, wincing as my ears popped.

It had been four months since the sea dragon awoke. Four months since the clan of Eyre Heights finally had answers and were able to mourn the women that had been kidnapped and killed. Whenever I saw Bonnie, I could see it still haunted her, and more often than not, she was gone hunting.

I'd had to fight for my life, and I'd nearly slipped away. But Rhyme's voice had been there, calling me back from the afterlife. My healing was slow and when the wind blew, I lost all feeling in my fingers and toes. My ears rang now and again, but otherwise I was whole, and most importantly, happy.

We lived out the remainder of winter in the security of the mountain, and when the first hint of spring danced in the air, we moved to the lowlands, to a home which swelled on top of a hillock overlooking the sea.

The ice had thawed after a time, with cracking booms and minor tremors, loud enough to frighten any sleeping babe. I'd stand outside and watch it sometimes, the miracle and glory of nature. It was so beautiful, it still made me catch my breath.

I'd learned a lot about myself through assisting the ice lords, and had had the opportunity to strengthen my friendship with Lessie. We lived within walking distance, and she was somehow, miraculously pregnant.

But it was Rhyme who made my heart beat faster every day.

"Phera?" His low voice rolled across the house.

Tugging on a robe but leaving my curls loose, I padded across the carpeted floors into the main room. "Summer is coming. I smelled it on the wind this morning."

Gray eyes crinkled around the edges as he smiled at me, then opened his arms. "Come here."

I was in his arms in a moment, resting my hands on his chest and lifting my face so he could kiss me.

He did with the slow fever I never grew tired of. A kiss of wonderment and love. His arms tightened around me and a new sensation washed over me—that I was lucky and had been granted a second chance, an opportunity I would not waste.

He murmured soft nothings in my ear, keeping me close to him. I studied his face, trailing my fingers down the length of his cheek and pausing when he captured my fingertips and kissed them.

"What is it?" I asked.

"I'm not sure how to tell you this, but I have news."

My heart skipped, because news might mean anything. In some regards, I still worried about the Academy of Mages and whether they'd send someone to check on me. My sentence had a time limit—ten years of serving the ice lords—so surely, one day, they'd return. But Rhyme's next words quelled my worries and stroked a hint of excitement.

"One of the neighboring clans heard of what happened here and would like our help."

I drew a slow breath. Finally, another challenge, another request for help. Not that I didn't enjoy relaxing in the lowlands, watching the sea, and making love to

Rhyme. But I'd healed, and magic sang within me, ready to be used.

"What's wrong?"

"They've captured a beast."

I lifted an eyebrow.

"A talking beast. Claims to know the future."

I sighed. "I wonder if it's the seer again. We should have captured her instead of leaving her in peace."

"There's only one way to find out."

"I'll pack our things."

"I've already saddled Rosie. She's ready to go. We'll stop by to see Isak and Lessie."

I squeezed his shoulders. "Surely they aren't coming."

He chuckled. "You won't be able to stop them."

I released him to go back, then spun around and flung myself into his arms again, holding tight. This was better, far better than anything I could have imagined.

Thanks for reading *Mage Bride* and taking a chance on this new romantasy. This is the beginning of a collection of standalone fantasy romances about brides who are betrayed and use magic to redeem themselves.

If you enjoyed the book and want more romance check out the *Tower Knights* collection for gothic-inspired fantasy romance featuring cursed knights.

Want more action/adventure and female warriors? Check out *Night of the Dark Fae* or *Gods & Goddess of Labraid*.

Curious about what's coming next? Stay tuned for *Pirate Bride*, coming Summer 2025.

**See all my books and enjoy a mystery discount on signed hardcovers when you visit my shop: angelajford.com**

# What to read next

Enjoyed this story but want more? Check out the Tower Knights collection: complete, stand-alone spicy fantasy romances.

Phantom of the Opera meets Beauty and the Beast in this gothic-inspired dark fantasy romance.

*A haunted tower, a mysterious instructor, and the lure of the music of the night...*

**Get a discount on signed hardcovers when you visit angelajford.com**

# Also by Angela J. Ford

Join my email list for updates, previews, giveaways, and new release notifications. Join now: www.angelajford.com/signup

## Tower Knights (fantasy romance)

*Gothic-inspired adult steamy fantasy romance. Each novel can be read as a standalone and features a different couple.*

## One Winter Night (fantasy romance)

*Winter-themed cozy fantasy romance with steampunk vibes. Each novel is a standalone and features a difference couple.*

## Betrayed Brides (fantasy romance)

*A collection of romantasy standalones featuring a bride who has been betrayed and uses magic to redeem herself.*

## Tales of the Enchanted Wildwood (fairy tale romance)

*Adult fairy tales blending fantasy action-adventure with steamy romance. Each short story can be read as a stand-alone and features a different couple.*

## Night of the Dark Fae Trilogy (romantic epic fantasy)

*A complete epic fantasy trilogy featuring a strong heroine, dark fae, orcs, goblins, dragons, antiheroes, magic, and romance.*

## Gods & Goddesses of Labraid (epic fantasy)

*A complete epic fantasy duology featuring a warrior princess with a dire future who embarks on a perilous quest to regain her fallen kingdom.*

## Lore of Nomadia Trilogy (epic fantasy)

*The story of an alluring nymph, a curious librarian, a renowned hunter, and a mad sorceress as they seek to save—or destroy—the empire of Nomadia.*

## Chronicles of the Four Worlds (epic fantasy)

*A complete six-book epic fantasy series spanning two hundred years, featuring an epic battle between mortals and immortals.*

## Legend of the Nameless One Series (epic fantasy)

*A complete five-book epic fantasy adventure series featuring an enchantress, a wizard, and a sarcastic dragon.*

Visit angelajford.com for signed books, exclusive book swag and luxe book boxes.

# About the Author

 Angela J. Ford is a bestselling author who writes epic fantasy and steamy fantasy romance with vivid worlds, gray characters and endings you just can't guess. She has written and published over 30 books.

Aside from writing she and her husband own The Signed Book Shop. A one-stop shop for readers to find signed books and book merchandise.

If you happen to be in Nashville, you'll most likely find her enjoying a white chocolate mocha and daydreaming about her next book.

facebook.com/angelajfordauthor

instagram.com/angelajfordbooks

amazon.com/Angela-J-Ford/e/B0052U9PZO

bookbub.com/authors/angela-j-ford